"*You were born to grandeur.*"

Grant's voice deepened. "The daughter of an earl. Journeying to the Outback is an escape for you. I could fall in love with you then you'd go off home to Daddy, back to your own world."

"So what's the solution?" Francesca was compelled to clutch him for support.

"Neither of us allows ourselves to get carried away," he said brusquely. "You're so beautiful. But I don't think your father would get a big kick out of knowing you were dallying with a rough-around-the-edges man from the Outback."

It in no way described him. "Rugged, Grant. Never rough. I like you. Temper and all. I like the way you hit on an idea and go for it. What I don't like is the way you see me as a threat."

He could see the hurt in her eyes but he was compelled to speak. "Because you *are* a threat, Francesca. A real threat. To us both."

Dear Reader,

Ever since I can remember, our legendary Outback has had an almost mystical grip on me. The cattlemen have become cultural heroes, figures of romance, excitement and adventure. These tough, dynamic, sometimes dangerous men carved out their destinies in this new world of Australia as they drove deeper and deeper into the uncompromising Wild Heart with its extremes of stark grandeur and bleached cruelty.

The type of man I like to write about is a unique and definable breed—rugged, masculine and full of vigor. This Outback man is strong yet sensitive, courageous enough to battle all the odds in order to claim the woman of his dreams.

The English Bride is the third of three linked books in which I explore the friendships, loves, rivalries and reconciliations between two great Australian pioneering families. They are truly LEGENDS OF THE OUTBACK.

Margaret Way

Each story can be read independently, but together they create an intimate family saga.

THE ENGLISH BRIDE

Margaret Way

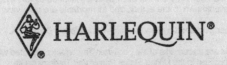

TORONTO • NEW YORK • LONDON
AMSTERDAM • PARIS • SYDNEY • HAMBURG
STOCKHOLM • ATHENS • TOKYO • MILAN • MADRID
PRAGUE • WARSAW • BUDAPEST • AUCKLAND

ISBN 0-373-03619-1

THE ENGLISH BRIDE

First North American Publication 2000.

Copyright © 2000 by Margaret Way, Pty., Ltd.

Visit us at www.eHarlequin.com

Printed in U.S.A.

CHAPTER ONE

IT WAS getting on towards late afternoon when Grant Cameron set the chopper down on the rear lawn of Kimbara as sweetly as a pelican setting down on a lagoon. Winds created by the whirling fanlike rotor stirred up a mini dust storm mixed with grass clippings and a sea of spent blossom from the nearby bauhinias but that quickly abated as the long blades wound to a standstill. Grant completed his interior checks and took off his headset, preparatory to jumping down onto the grass.

This was historic Kimbara Station, desert stronghold of the Kinross family since the early days of settlement; the nearest neighbour to his own family station, Opal Downs, some hundred miles to the north-east.

His older brother, Rafe, much loved and much respected, was currently on honeymoon in the United States with his new bride and love of his life, Alison Cameron, nee Kinross. Rafe ran the station. He, Grant, was making a very successful business out of his own aerial mustering service, operating out of Opal. It had suited both brothers well. Rafe was the cattleman. He was the pilot.

He'd always been mad about aircraft even since he'd been a kid. Even the inconsolable grief of losing their beloved parents to a light aircraft crash hadn't killed his love of flying. With an outback so vast flying was a way of life in Australia. The tragedy had to be survived.

Grant reached for his akubra and slung it on at an unconsciously rakish angle. The sun still had a powerful kick in it and he couldn't altogether forget his tawny colouring, a Cameron trademark. "A pride of lions" was the way people used to describe his dad, Douglas Cameron, and his two sons, Rafe and Grant.

A pride of lions!

For a moment a terrible sadness constricted his chest. He wished with all his heart his dad was still alive. Mum and Dad. They never got to see him make such a success of himself. They would have been proud. He had always been the younger brother, a bit of a wildcat trying to develop in his brother's shadow. Rafe was born responsible, ready to take over from their father.

Out of the helicopter Grant made a quick circuit of the aircraft, his eyes always checking for the slightest sign of possible trouble though the fleet was scrupulously maintained. The yellow fuselage with its broad blue stripe and company logo in blue and gold gave off a crackle as the metal cooled down. He patted the insignia with satisfaction and made off for the house.

It had been an exhausting day driving a whole heap of cantankerous, overheated cattle in from the isolated Sixty Mile out near Jarajara, a single huge sentinel granite dome that marked Kimbara's western border to the camp Brod's men had set up out near Mareeba Waters with its winding water courses. Camp would be shifted as the muster went on. The men were expected to be out for the best past of three weeks. What he needed now was a long cold beer and to feast his tired eyes on a beautiful woman.

Francesca

Not necessarily in that order he thought dryly. Francesca was occupying far too many of his thoughts these days. Lady Francesca de Lyle, first cousin to Brod Kinross, master of Kimbara and brother to Ally, his new sister-in-law. Cameron and Kinross were legendary names in this part of the world, pioneering giants.

Now with the marriage of Rafe and Alison the two families were finally united to everyone's great satisfaction except maybe Lainie Rhodes of Victoria Springs who had nurtured an outsize crush on Rafe since puberty struck her. Not that Lainie wasn't good marriage material but there had never been anyone else for Rafe but his Ally.

The unbreakable bond between them had been forged in their childhood out of tempered steel. Now they were man and wife, deliriously happy from all accounts but Grant realised full well he had better start making plans.

Big as Opal's homestead was he had no intention of intruding on his brother's and Ally's privacy. They would want the homestead to themselves no matter how much they tried to reassure him Opal was as much his home as theirs. A big *share* of Opal Station maybe, which had financed his aerial muster business, but the homestead was for the newlyweds. He was determined on that. Besides Ally had lots of plans for doing the place up and he guessed it needed it.

What would it be like to be married? Grant mused as he strode past the original old kitchens and servants' quarters. Long out-of-date they were perfectly maintained for their historic value. Shrubs surrounded these outbuildings, light filtering trees, the whole linked to the Big House by the long covered walkway he now took.

What would it be like to come home each night to

a woman he could take to his heart, to his bed? A woman to share his hopes and dreams, his profoundest inner expectations. A woman he belonged with as surely as she belonged with him.

The first time he met Francesca de Lyle when he was in his teens he had felt an instant click, a deep rapport, now years later he was well into fantasising about her. Why then was he so persuaded an intimate relationship with Francesca could only bring danger to them both? Maybe he wasn't ready for any deep relationship after all. Hell, wasn't he too damned busy to commit. Nothing should be on his mind but work. Building up the business. He had such ideas.

A branch of Cameron Airways was now carrying mail and freight but he'd had recent discussions in Brisbane the state capital a good thousand miles away, with Drew Forsythe of Trans Continental Resources regarding building a helicopter fleet for use in minerals, oil and natural gas exploration.

He'd met the very high profile Forsythe and his beautiful wife, Eve, on several occasions but that was the first time they'd ever got into really talking business. And he had Francesca of all people to thank for that.

Never one, apparently, to let a good public relations opportunity go by, Francesca who had struck an immediate chord with the Forsythes when they had all been seated together at a charity banquet had brought up the idea in the course of an enjoyable evening.

Beautiful blue eyes sparkling she put it to Forsythe: "Doesn't this make good sense to you? Grant knows the Interior like the back of his hand and he's absolutely committed to the big picture, isn't that right, Grant?" She had leaned back towards him then, so heart stoppingly graceful in her strapless satin gown, her lovely cool, clear English voice, full of support and encouragement. Ah, the bright aura of breeding and privilege!

And she was clever. If some sort of a deal ever came off, and he was working on it right now, he owed her. A glorious romantic weekend away together, he fantasised. One of those jewel-like Barrier Reef islands that had those luxurious little self-contained bungalows down near the beach. Though he would have to watch her in the hot Queensland sun. She had the flawless porcelain complexion that so often set off Titian hair. How strange she should want to fit into his background on the fringe of the great desert heart. It was almost like trying to grow an exquisite pink rosebush on the banks of a dried-up clay pan. For all his deep and immediate attraction to her they were an impossible match. And he better not lose sight of it.

He lost sight of it less than two minutes later when Francesca herself appeared, running down the side verandah and leaning over the white wrought-iron balustrade wreathed with a prolific lilac trumpeted vine that gave off a seductive fragrance in the golden heat.

"Grant!" she called, waving happily. "How lovely to see you. Of course I heard the chopper." A singing sweetness showed in every line of her body. Sweetness and excitement.

"Come here," he ordered very gently as he came alongside, reaching up a long arm to pull her lovely head down to him. Despite all the little lectures he gave himself, despite all natural caution, every atom of his being was focused on kissing her. He even murmured her name unknowingly as he put his mouth over hers, sensation beating through him like the powerful whoosh of a rotor. What in hell made him do it? But he was a man and keenly physical.

When he let her go she was breathless, trying not to tremble, a deep pink colour running across the fine skin of her cheeks, sparkling lights in the depths of her eyes. Her beautiful flame-coloured hair had come loose from its clasp and spilled around her face and over her shoulders. "That's some greeting!" Her voice was little more than a soft tremble.

"You shouldn't look at me that way," he warned, still feeling ripples of pleasure moving down through his body, pooling in his loins.

"What way?" She gave a shaky laugh, feeling enslaved by his enormous dash, moving back along the wide verandah as he resumed his journey to the front of the house.

"*You* know, Francesca," he half growled, half mocked. "Lord are you a sight for sore eyes!" He ran his gaze over her, from the tip of her radiant head to her toes. His hazel eyes, which could turn grey or green according to his mood, were now a clear green beneath the brim of his black akubra. They scanned her face, her swan's neck, the slender body with its willow waist, her light limbs, a muscle in his hard jaw lightly flicking.

It was impossible to cast his glance away so caught up was he in her feminine beauty, the soft ravishing prettiness he found irresistible. She was wearing riding gear. Such riding gear! The aristocratic young English lady from the grand stately home and one of the most egalitarian young women he had ever known.

Her short-sleeved cream silk blouse lightly skimmed her delicate breasts and was tucked into tight-fitting cream jodhpurs. Highly polished, very expensive, tan coloured riding boots adorned her small feet. There wasn't an ounce of excess weight on her. She had the neatest, sleekest little butt and good straight legs. It nearly mesmerised him just to see her move along the verandah, near dancing to keep up with him. To his overheated mind, and body, make no mistake about it it thrummed like electricity, she appeared to be floating, so lightly were her feet touching the timber floorboards.

"A hard day?" Francesca asked him as he mounted the short flight of stone steps to the verandah, excited, not her usual calm, contained self at all.

He leaned against the rail with slouching elegance, smiling at her with the unblinking cat's eyes she found so wildly attractive. "I'm over it now I've seen you," he drawled. He was, too. "What have you been doing with yourself all day?"

"Come and I'll tell you." She indicated the comfortable white wicker furniture. "I expect you'd like a cold beer? Brod always does."

He nodded and took off his hat using it like a Frisbee to skim unerringly onto the head of a wooden sculpture.

"Rebecca will be here in a moment," Francesca slid into the chair he held out for her. Rebecca was mistress of Kimbara, Brod's new wife. "We've been organising a picnic race meeting for most of the day. We thought it would be a change from the usual polo. Rebecca worries about Brod when he plays. He's such a daredevil. For that matter so are you." She actually shivered at some of her recollections. Polo was a dangerous game. Especially the way these fellows played it.

"So you worry about me as well?" He held her with his eyes.

"I worry about you *all*," she returned lightly before she drowned in his expression. It struck her more than ever how physically alike Grant and his brother Rafe were. The rangy height, the golden good looks, though Grant was tawnier.

Both had great presence. Both wore achievement like a badge. If there were a difference, Rafe had a kind of courtliness about him. There was no other word for it. Grant showed more "temper" a high mettled energy and determination that didn't sit all that comfortably with everyone. To put it in a nutshell Grant Cameron could be difficult. Add to that, he had a habit of speaking his mind, without holding back. He was full of energy and had a macho quality, an absolute manliness that characterised these men of the outback. In some respects he even seemed like a creature from another world. A creature of vast open spaces with no boundaries. The image of a splendid young lion sat easily on him. He was her first taste of a thrilling excitement that contained a kernel of caution. She knew her feelings for Grant Cameron were getting right out of hand.

Now he knit his dark golden brows together, staring across at her, his strong brown arms on the circular glass-topped table steely with muscle. He was wearing the uniform of his company in serviceable khaki the blue and gold logo on the breast pocket. He looked great, the afternoon breeze ruffling his thick tawny hair with its pronounced deep wave.

"So what's the verdict, my lady?" He came closer to grasping her hand. Never letting her go.

She laughed and blushed at the same time. "Was I staring? Sorry. I was just thinking how much alike you and Rafe are. Growing more so as you—"

"Mature?" he cut in swiftly, his relaxed easy drawl taking on a faint glittery edge.

"Oh, Grant," she said in gentle reproach. Francesca knew the brothers were devoted to each other, but Grant a couple of years younger must have chafed often under Rafe's authority. With both parents dead Rafe had had to take on almost a parental role from an early age. Grant still had a tendency to chafe if only because of his driving ambition to prove himself, to be the man his father always said he would be. Grant fairly pulsed with raw ambition, undischarged energy. "Actually I was going to say, as you grow older," she told him mildly, watching his tall, super lean body with its athlete's muscles relax.

"Of course you were," he agreed with his charming, slightly crooked smile that revealed perfect white teeth. "Sometimes, Francesca, I've got a perverse devil in me."

"Yes, I know," she told him gently.

"I love Rafe as much as any brother could."

"I know you do," she said with understanding, "and I know what you mean so don't bother explaining." The best of relationships were fraught with little tensions. Like mother and daughter. She turned her head as footsteps sounded in the front hall. "That'll be Rebecca."

A moment later Rebecca appeared like a summer breeze, all smiles, touching Francesca affectionately on the shoulder before speaking directly to Grant who came swiftly to his feet. "Don't bother to get up, Grant," she said, realising he must be tired. "All over for the day?"

"Thank the Lord." He gave a wry grin.

"Then you could probably do with a cold beer?"

He laughed aloud and resumed his seat. "Brod sure has his womenfolk trained. Francesca has just offered me one, too. That'd be great, Rebecca. I have to admit it was long, hard and dusty. I'm parched." He was struck again at how much Rebecca had changed from the enigmatic young woman who had first come to Kimbara to write Fee Kinross's biography. Fee, Francesca's mother, had had a brilliant career on the London stage. The biography was due out any day.

Since her marriage to Brod, Rebecca was all friendliness and warmth, happiness and contentment shining out of her quite extraordinary grey eyes. This was a marriage that would work, he thought with great satisfaction. God knows Brod and Ally had one hell of a childhood with their arrogant bastard of a father. Such was Rafe's persona even Stewart Kinross had approved of Rafe, though he hadn't lived to see Rafe and his only daughter, Alison, married.

Grant was certain Kinross would never have approved of him. "Too much the hothead!" Kinross had once described him, "with the intolerable habit of expressing his quite juvenile opinions." Opinions, of course, that ran counter to the lordly Kinross. Still the two families, Cameron and Kinross had always been entwined. Almost kin. Now they were.

When Rebecca returned with his cold beer, just the one—he was too responsible a pilot to consider another—and an iced tea for herself and Francesca, they talked family matters, their latest communications from Rafe and Ally, local gossip, what Fee and David Westbury, the visiting first cousin to Francesca'a aristocratic father, were up to. The two had become inseparable to the extent Francesca told them she wouldn't be surprised to get a phone call to say they'd popped into the register office that very day. Which would make Fee's third attempt at making a go of marriage.

They were still talking about Fee and the important cameo role she was to play in a new Australian movie, when they were interrupted by the shrilling of the phone, the latest miracle for the outback that had depended for so long on radio communication. Rebecca went to answer it, returning with an expression that wiped all the laughter from her luminous grey eyes. "It's for you, Grant, Bob Carlton." She named his second-in-charge. "One of the fleet hasn't reached base camp or called in, either. Bob sounded a bit concerned. Take it in Brod's study."

"Thanks, Rebecca." Grant rose to his impressive lean height. "Did he say which station?"

"Oh I'm sorry!" Rebecca touched her creamy forehead in self-reproach. "I should have told you at once. It's Bunnerong."

The station was even more remote than they were. About sixty miles to the north-west. Grant made his way through the Kinross homestead, familiar to him from childhood. It was amazingly grand in contrast to the Cameron stronghold with its quietly fading Victorian gentility. Ally, of course, would change all that. Ally the whirlwind but for now his mind was on what Bob had to say.

Bob, in his mid-fifties, was a great bloke. A great organiser, a great mechanic, well liked by everyone. Grant relied on him, but Bob was a born worrier, a firm believer in Murphy's Law, whereby anything that could go wrong, would. Equally Bob was determined no harm would come to any of "his boys."

On the phone Grant received Bob's assurance all necessary checks had been made and the chopper had passed the mandatory 100-hour service. The helicopter was to have set down when the stockmen were camped at Bunnerong's out station at approximately four o'clock. The pilot, a good one with plenty of experience in aerial muster had not arrived by four forty-five when Bunnerong contacted Bob by radio. Bob in turn had not been able to contact the pilot by company radio frequency.

"I wouldn't worry too much about it." Grant wasn't overly concerned at that point.

"You know me, Grant, I'm going to," Bob answered. "It's not like Curly. He runs by an inbuilt timetable."

"Sure," Grant acknowledged. "But you know as well as I do things can go wrong with the radio. It's not all that unusual. It's happened to me. Besides it's almost dusk. Curly would have put down somewhere and made camp for the night. He's got all he needs to make himself comfortable. He'd resume again at first light. If he's anything like me he's dog-tired. Besides, he's not actually due to start the muster until morning anyway."

All of which was true. "There's an hour or so of light left," Grant said at length breaking in on Bob. "I'll take the chopper up and have a look around, though I'm coming from another direction. I need to refuel on Kimbara, if I'm going to get close in to Bunnerong."

"I suppose we might as well wait for morning," Bob sighed. "Curly could still turn up. Bunnerong can get a message to us and I'll relay it to you."

So it was decided. "Curly" to all because of a single wisp of hair that curled like a baby's on his bald patch, was a pro. He had food with him. A swag. He'd probably put down near a bush lagoon and set up camp for the night. Nevertheless Grant felt the responsibility to take his chopper up. Initiate a bit of a search before night fell.

Bob's mood had affected him, he thought wryly. Experience told him Curly, though obviously having problems with his radio was most likely safe and sound setting up camp on the ground. Still he liked to know *exactly* where every one of his pilots and helicopters in service were.

Grant walked swiftly back through the house, telling the two young women of his intentions the moment he set foot on the verandah.

"Why don't you let me come with you?" Francesca asked quickly, keen to help if she could. "You know what they say, two pairs of eyes are better than one."

Rebecca nodded in agreement. "I was able to help Brod once on a search and rescue. You remember?"

"That was from the Beech Baron," Grant told her, a shade repressively. "Francesca isn't used to helicopters. The way they fly, the heat and the noise. She could very easily get airsick."

Francesca stood away from her chair. "I don't suffer from motion sickness at all, Grant. In the air. On the water. Please take me. I want to help if I can."

His response wasn't all that she hoped. The expression in his hazel eyes suggested there was a decided possibility she could become a liability. But in the end he nodded in laconic permission. "All right, lady! Let's go."

Minutes later the rotor was roaring and they were lifting vertically from the lawn, rising well above the line of trees, climbing, then steering away for the desert fringe. Francesca like Grant was strapped into her co-pilot seat, wearing earphones that at least made the loud noise of the swishing blades tolerable. Still she found it a thrilling experience to be up in the air looking down at the vast wilderness with all the rock formations undergoing another change in their astonishing colour display. Even when they flew through thermal cross-winds over the desert she kept her cool as the winds took hold of the small aircraft and shook it so it plunged into a short, sickening dive.

"O.K.?" Grant spoke through the headphones, a deep frown of concern between his eyes.

"Aye, aye, skipper!" She lifted her right hand in a parody of a smart salute. Did he really think she was going to go to pieces like the ladies of old? Have the vapours? She had pioneering blood in her veins as well. Her maternal ancestor had been Ewan Kinross, a legendary cattle king. The fact that she had been reared in the ordered calm of the beautiful English countryside and her exclusive boarding school didn't mean she hadn't inherited the capacity to face a far more dangerous way of life. Besides it was as she'd told him. She had a cast iron stomach and she was too excited for nerves. She wanted to learn this way of life. She wanted to learn all about Grant Cameron's life.

They searched until it got to the point when they had to turn back. When they landed Brod was waiting for them in the brief mauve dusk that in moments would turn to a darkness that was literally pitch black.

"No luck?" Brod asked as Grant jumped out onto the grass turning to catch Francesca by the waist and swing her down like the featherweight she was.

"If Curly doesn't turn up on Bunnerong first thing

in the morning we're looking at another search. Bob report in?''

"No news. Nothing.'' Brod shook his head. "You'll stay the night.'' It wasn't a question but a statement of fact. "Better you're here anyway. We're closer to Bunnerong if there's any need of a search. I expect your man is boiling the billy now moaning his radio is out of order.''

"I shouldn't be surprised,'' Grant responded to Brod's good spirits. "It's Francesca here who's the real surprise.''

"How so?'' Brod turned to smile down on his English cousin, as dark with his raven hair and tanned skin as Grant was tawny gold.

"I think he thought I was going to go into a panic when we hit some thermals,'' Francesca explained lightly, striking Grant's arm in reproach.

"I wouldn't have blamed you if you did,'' he answered with a faintly teasing smile, enjoying fending her off. "I've always said you're much more than a pretty face.'' A ravishingly pretty face.

"It would take a lot to put Fran in a tizzy,'' Brod said with affection. "We've learnt over the years this little piece of English china has plenty of spunk.''

Up at the homestead Rebecca smilingly allotted him a guest room overlooking the rear of the house. The meandering creek that ran near and encircled the home compound revealed itself in a silver line as the moon turned on its radiance. Brod walked in a few minutes later with a pile of clean, soap-smelling clothes from his own wardrobe.

"Here, these should fit,'' he announced, placing the clothes neatly on the bed, a blue-and-white striped cotton shirt on top, cotton beige trousers and underwear that hadn't even come out of its packet by the look of it. Both men were much the same height a few inches over six feet with the lean, powerful physique of the super active.

"Am I glad of them. Thanks a lot," Grant answered, turning away from his own speculation of the night to smile at his brother's best friend. With Rafe and Brod those few years older he'd always been the one trying to catch up, trying to catch them, trying to emulate their achievements, academically and on the sports field. All in all he hadn't done too badly.

"No problem." There was an answering smile in Brod's eyes. "You've saved me dozens of times. I'm for a long, hot shower. I expect you are, too. It's been a thoroughly tiring day." He started to move off then stopped briefly at the door. "By the way I don't think I thanked you properly for doing such a great job," he said with evident approval. "It's not just the way you handle the chopper, which is brilliant, you're a cattleman as well. The combination makes you extraordinarily good."

"Thanks, mate." Grant grinned. "I aim to offer the very best service. And it doesn't come cheap as you're due to find out. What time are we off in the morning always supposing Curly gets a message through he's okay?"

Brod frowned, answering a little vaguely for him. "Not as early as today, that's for sure. The men have their orders. They'll have plenty to do. We'll wait and see what the morning brings. I know bush logic tells us Curly has landed safely, but I'd like to stick around until we're sure."

"I appreciate that, Brod." Grant accepted his friend's support. "A land search in such a huge area would be out of the question. It will take aircraft to find him if he's in any kind of trouble.''

''Not that it's odd having problems with the radio,'' Brod echoed Grant's own previous words, obviously trying to offer reassurance mixed in with the voice of long experience. Brod's expression brightened. ''Now, what about a barbeque? I feel like eating outdoors tonight and it gives me the opportunity to show off. I cook a great steak if I say so myself. We can throw in a few roast potatoes. The girls can whip up a salad. What more could a man want?''

Grant smiled broadly. ''Go for it! I'm hungry enough to eat the best steak Kimbara can offer.''

''You're going to get it,'' Brod assured him.

A long, hot shower was a wonderful luxury after the heat and uproar of the day. The bellowing of the cattle as they were herded into doing what they clearly didn't want to do; leave the familiar surroundings of the scrub was still in his ears. More of the same tomorrow. And the day after. But he planned on getting right out of fieldwork. He wanted to concentrate on expanding the business. He'd go on building up the fleet and the team but his mind was firmly on extending the range of services.

With time on his hands and glad of the company of such good friends, he used some of the shampoo he found in the cupboard beneath the basin. Kinross sure knew how to look after its guests, he thought with wry admiration. There was an impressive array of stuff to make a guest feel good. Fancy soaps, bath gels, shower gels, body lotion, talc, toothbrushes, toothpaste, hair dryer, electric shaver. Lots of good, big absorbent towels. Man-size. Brilliant!

He stepped out of the shower and wrapped one

around himself, feeling the exhaustions of the day slip away. His hair needed cutting as usual. Barbers weren't all that easy to come by in the desert. He shook his wet, darkened hair like a seal deciding he'd better use the dryer if he wanted to look presentable.

Which he did. He was intensely aware of his attraction to Francesca, her marvellous drawing power though he knew how ill advised it was. The Camerons and the Kinrosses had always lived like desert lords but their world was beyond "civilisation" as Lady Francesca de Lyle knew it. No question the call of the outback had reached her. After all she had an Australian mother born in this very house but Francesca was on holiday, taking the rose-coloured holiday view. It was impossible for her to realise the day-to-day isolation, the terrible battles that were fought against drought, flood and heat, accident, tragic deaths. Men could bear the loneliness, the struggles and frustrations, the crushing workload. He knew in his heart an English rose like Francesca would find it all unbearable no matter how adaptable she claimed she was. She simply had no experience of the bush and the hazards it presented.

Grant threw down the hair dryer, thinking he shouldn't have used it. It made his hair look positively *wild*. He turned to dressing, pulling out the belt of his uniform to thread it through the cotton trousers. No difficulty with sizing. The fit was perfect. If only he were certain Curly was safe and sound he could really look forward to enjoying this evening.

It had been lonely at home with Rafe away on honeymoon. He was looking forward to a letter from them or maybe another phone call. Ally had been so full of their stay in New York. She adored it. The excitement she felt as she "hit the sidewalk" the "thrum" of the place more electric than any other city on earth. "And we've got you some wonderful presents," she'd added. "Really special!" That was Ally and she had the money.

The Camerons had never kept pace with the Kinrosses in the generation of great wealth, though Opal was an industry leader and Rafe was dead set on expansion, building up a chain, just as he, himself, was determined on making his mark in aviation.

The pride of lions! Well he and Rafe had tasted tragedy as had Brod and Ally. At least some things were now working out. Brod had found real love, much rarer than people thought. As for Rafe and Ally! They were like two sides of the same coin. Allowing himself to fall in love with Francesca had to make him downright crazy. Easy enough to get led astray, though, he reasoned. Finding the path back might prove very, very, difficult.

Francesca was crossing through the front hall when Grant descended the stairs. She looked up feeling a sudden rush of blood to her face. He looked marvellous, his strong, handsome features relaxed, hazel eyes sparkling, his full, thick head of hair, obviously freshly washed, settling into the deep natural waves women paid a fortune to achieve. She was astonished at her own desire, so sweet, so primitive like a woman staring at the man she wanted for her perfect mate.

"Hi!" His voice was pitched thrillingly low, stirring her further.

She had to force a flippant tone in case he read what was on her mind and man-like backed off. "You look *cool.*"

"Courtesy Brod." He grinned. "He rustled up some gear."

"It suits you." She spoke with a nice balance of admiration and teasing.

"Actually you look very sweet yourself." His eyes gently mocked. She was wearing a sapphire-blue full skirt with a matching strappy little top, the fabric printed with white hibiscus. Blue sandals almost the same shade were on her feet, her Titian hair wound into some braided coil that suited her beautifully. He saw the apricot flush on her creamy skin. He knew it was there because he was coming close.

How did it happen? This longing for a woman that sent a man reeling? He'd been making love to her in his mind at least three times a week for some time now, seriously considering it *had* to happen, shocked because he couldn't seem to come to his senses. But what did sense have to do with sexual attraction? He felt compelled to have an affair. He couldn't make the wider choice, yet he moved right up to her, surprising her and himself by moving her into an impromptu tango, remembering how they had danced and danced at Brod's then Rafe's wedding.

There was music in him, Francesca thought. Music, rhythm, a sensuality that was reducing her limbs to jelly. This man was taking her over utterly, making all her senses bloom like a flower.

"I'm in perfect company right now," he murmured in her ear, just barely resisting the temptation to take the pink earlobe into his mouth.

"Me, too." The words just slipped out, very soft but not concealing her intensity. She hadn't made a conscious decision to fall in love with him surely, but his effect on her was so pervasive she could hardly bear to contemplate her holiday on Kimbara coming to an end.

Rebecca, coming to find them, burst into spontaneous applause at the considerable panache of their dance. "You're naturals, both of you," she cried. "I've never thought of it before but this is a terrific dance floor." She looked around the very spacious front hall, speculation in her eyes.

"Why would you need it when you've got the old ballroom?" Francesca asked, catching her breath as Grant whirled her into a very close stop.

"I mean for Brod and me," Rebecca smiled, still very much the bride. "Come and join us for a drink. I've chilled a seriously good Riesling. It's beautiful out on the back verandah. The air is filled with the scent of boronia. How I love it. The stars are out in their zillions." She came forward very happily to link her arm through Francesca's, her long, gleaming dark ribbon of hair falling softly from a centre parting the way her husband loved it, the skirt of her summery white dress fluttering in the breeze that blew through the open doorway.

They found Brod wrapped in a professional-looking apron, the large brick barbeque well alight, the potatoes in foil already cooking. Ratatouille kebabs prepared by Rebecca lay ready for the grill plate, a leafy green walnut and mushroom salad prepared by Francesca waiting for the dressing.

Grant was given the enjoyable task of opening the wine, and pouring it into the tulip-shaped glasses set out on the long table, while Francesca passed around the crackers spread with a smoked salmon paté she had processed a half hour before. It was light and luscious and the conversation began to flow. These were people, interconnected through family, who genuinely enjoyed one another's company. The steaks, prime Kimbara beef, were set to sizzle over the hot coals and Rebecca decided she'd like a tarragon wine sauce so went to the kitchen to fetch it. While they were waiting, Grant walked Francesca to the very edge of the verandah so they could see the moon reflected in the glassy-smooth surface of the creek.

"Such a heavenly night," she breathed, lifting her head from contemplation of the silvery waters to the glittering heavens. "The Southern Cross is always over the tip of the house. It's so easy to pick out."

Grant nodded. "Rafe and Ally won't see it in the United States. The cross is gradually shifting southward in the sky."

"Is it really?" Francesca turned her head to stare up at him, thrilled because he was so *tall*.

"It is, my lady." He gave a mocking bow. "A result of the earth's precession or the circular motion of the earth's axis. The Southern Cross was known to the people of the ancient world, Babylonians and Greeks. They thought it part of the constellation Centaurus. See the star furthest to the south?" He pointed it out.

"The brightest?"

He nodded. "A star of the first magnitude. It points to the South Pole. The aborigines have wonderful Dreamtime legends about the Milky Way and stars. I'll tell you some of them one of these days. Maybe nights when we're camping out."

"Are you serious?"

A short silence. "I suppose it could be arranged." His voice sounded sardonic. "Do you think it would be a good idea, the two of us camping out under the stars?"

"I think it could be wonderful." Francesca drew a breath of sheer excitement.

"What about when the dingoes started to howl?" he mocked.

"Mournful not to say eerie cries, I know—" she shivered a little remembering "—but I'd have you to protect me."

"And who's going to protect me?" Suddenly he put a finger beneath her chin, turning up her face to him.

"Am I so much to worry about?" She cut to the very heart of the matter.

"I think so, yes," he answered slowly. "You're out of reach, Francesca."

"And I thought you were a man who aimed for the stars?" she taunted him very gently.

"Aircraft are safer than women," he countered dryly. "They don't preoccupy a man's mind."

"So that makes harmless little me a great danger?" Her voice was low-pitched but uniquely intense.

"Except in the realm of my secret dreams," he surprised himself by admitting.

It was a tremendous turn-on, causing Francesca's body to quiver like a plucked string. "That's very revealing, Grant. Why would you reveal so much of yourself to me?" she asked in some frustration.

"Because in many ways we're intensely compatible. I think we knew that very early on."

"When we were just teenagers?" There was simply no way she could deny it. "And now we're to assume a different relationship?"

"Not assume, my lady." His voice deepened, became somewhat combative. "You were born to grandeur. The daughter of an earl. Journeying to the outback is in lots of ways an escape for you, maybe even an escape from reality. An attempt to avoid much of the pressure from your position in life. I'd expect your father will confidently expect you to marry a man from within your own ranks. A member of the English aristocracy. At the very least a scion of one of the established families.''

It was perfectly true. Her father had certain hopes of her. Even two possible suitors. ''I'm Fee's daughter, too.'' She tried to stave the issue off. ''That makes me half Australian. Fee only wants me to be happy.''

''Which means I'm right. Your father has high expectations of you. He wouldn't want to lose you.''

Francesca shook her head almost pleadingly. ''Daddy will never lose me. I love him. But he has his own life you know.''

''But no grandchildren.'' Grant pointed out bluntly. ''You have to give him them. Such a child, a male child, would become his heir. The future Earl of Moray. Inescapably a fact.''

''Oh don't let's take that all on yet, Grant,'' Francesca burst out. She wanted them to be together, with no conflicts between them.

But Grant had other ideas, seeing where it was taking them. ''I have to. You know as well as I do we're becoming increasingly involved. Hell what am *I* sacrificing here? I could fall in love with you then you'd go off home to Daddy, back to your own world, leaving me to profound wretchedness.''

Somehow she didn't associate him with becoming any woman's victim. He was too much the self-contained *man*. ''I think you have what it takes to resist me.''

''Darn right!'' Abruptly he bent his head and gave her a hard kiss. ''I've seen these patterns before.''

"So what's the solution?" She was compelled to clutch him for support.

"Neither of us allows ourselves to get carried away," he said brusquely.

"So much for your behaviour then. Why do you have to kiss me?"

He laughed, a low, attractive sound with a hint of self-disgust. "That's the hell of it, Francesca. Reconciling sexual desire with the need for good sense."

"So sadly there are to be no more kisses?" she challenged with a little note of scepticism.

He looked down into her light filled eyes, aware of the complexity of his feelings. She looked so lovely, very much a piece of porcelain, a woman to be cherished, protected from damage. "Can I help it if I'm continually at war?" he asked ironically. "You're so beautiful, aren't you? You moved into my path like a princess from a fairy tale. I know dozens of eligible, available women. Wouldn't I be the world's biggest fool to pick on someone like you? A young woman who has lived a charmed life? Equally well I don't think your father would get a big kick out of knowing you were dallying with a rough-around-the-edges man from the outback."

It in no way described him. "Rugged, Grant. Never rough. You're a lot more edgy than Rafe, but he's very much your brother and one of the most courteous men I've ever met."

"Free from my aggression, you mean." Grant nodded in wry amusement. "It's an inborn grace, Francesca, he inherited from our father. I'm nowhere near as simpatico."

Her normally sweet voice was a little tart in her

throat, like citrus peel in chocolate. "Well don't feel too badly. *I* like you. Temper and all. I like the way you hit on an idea and go for it. I like your breadth of vision. I like the way you make big plans. I even like your strong sense of competitiveness. What I don't like is the way you see me as a threat."

He could see the hurt in her eyes but he was compelled to speak. "Because you *are* a threat, Francesca. A real threat. To us both."

"That's awful." She looked away abruptly over the moon-drenched home gardens.

"I know," he muttered sombrely, "but it makes sense."

Unlike a lot of men let loose at a barbeque, Brod cooked the steaks to perfection, each to their requirements from medium rare to well done. For all her whirring feelings Francesca enjoyed herself, eating a good meal, warming to the conversation, and afterwards offering to make coffee.

"I'll help you." Impulsively Grant moved back his chair, willing the pleasure of the evening to go on. Brod and Rebecca had shifted seats and were now holding hands. The younger couple wouldn't be missed for a while.

In the huge kitchen outfitted for feeding an army, Grant thought, Francesca set him to grinding the coffee beans, the marvellous aroma rising and flowing out towards them. Francesca was busy setting out cups and saucers then assembling plates for the slices of chocolate torte she'd already cut. All very deftly, he noticed. She was very organised, very methodical, with quick, neat hands.

"You're managing very well," he drawled.

"What is that supposed to mean?" The overhead light turned her glorious hair to flame, giving him a great wave of pleasure.

"Have you ever actually cooked a meal?" he smiled.

"I made the salad," she pointed out collectedly.

"And it was very good, but I can't think you ever have any need to go into a kitchen and start cooking the supper."

She scarcely remembered being allowed in the kitchen except at Christmas to stir the pudding. "Not at Ormond, no." She named her father's stately home. "We always had a housekeeper, Mrs. Lincoln. She was pretty fierce. Nothing casual about her and she had staff, just as Brod's father did, only Brod and Rebecca have decided they want to be on their own. At least for a while. Once I shifted to London to start work I managed to get all my own meals. It truly isn't difficult," she added dryly.

"When you weren't going out?" He poured boiling water into the plunger. "You must accept lots and lots of invitations?"

"I have a full social life." She flashed him a blue, sparkling look. "But it's not an obsession."

"No love affairs?" He found he couldn't bear the thought of her with another man.

"One or two romantic involvements. Like *you*." Grant Cameron didn't lack female admirers.

"No one serious?" he persisted as though the thought was gnawing away at him.

"I've yet to meet my perfect man," she answered sweetly.

"Which brings me to why you have designs on me." His effrontery took her breath away. "You can haul yourself out when the going gets tough. Because I'm only following my own instincts. You do have a certain emotional pull and physically you're extraordinarily attractive.''

He gave a mock bow, surprisingly elegant. ''Thank you, Francesca. That makes my heart swell.''

''As long as it's not your *head*,'' she retorted crisply.

''My head has the high ground at the moment,'' he drawled. ''But I've enjoyed tonight. Brod and Rebecca are such good company and you are *you*.''

It was so disconcerting, the swings from sarcastic to sizzling emotion. An acknowledgment, perhaps, that their connection was powerful, though he was going to fight it all the way.

''That's good I've done something right,'' Francesca said in response, trying to keep her tone light, but she was utterly confounded when tears came into her eyes. Being with him made her more sensitive, more womanly with a much bigger capacity for being hurt. For all the calmness of her voice, Grant was instantly alerted. He glanced up swiftly, catching her the moment before she blinked furiously.

''Francesca!'' Heart drumming with dismay and desire he reached for her, pulling her into his arms. ''What is it? Have I hurt you? I'm a brute. I'm sorry.'' He could see the pulse beating in her creamy throat answering the pulses that were beating in him. ''I'm trying to see what's best for both of us. Surely you can understand that?''

''Of course.'' Her voice was a husky whisper. She dashed her hand across her eyes. Just like a little girl. Grace under fire.

An immense wave of passion tied to a deep sense of protectiveness broke across him, causing him to mould her into him more tightly, achingly aware of the feel of her delicate breasts against the wall of his chest. He was on the verge of losing it. It was terrible. But good. Better than good. Ravishing.

She attempted to speak but he was seized by the urgent need to kiss her, to take the crushed strawberry sweetness of her mouth, to find her tongue, to move it back and forth against his in the age-old mating ritual. This incredible delight in a woman was something new to him. Something well beyond his former sexual experiences. He wanted her. Needed her like a man needs water.

There was tremendous passion in his kiss, a touch of fierceness that thrilled her because she knew she meant more to him than he dared acknowledge. His hand held her nape, cupped it, holding her head to him. She was almost lying back in his arms, allowing him to take his intense pleasure, and something deep, deep inside her started to melt. She was almost fainting under the tumult of sensation, her own ardent response. She had never known such intimacy, never before revelled in it, knowing it could be a cause of much unhappiness but she was too needy or too stupid to care.

What bright spirit impelled towards delight was ever known to figure out the cost?

They broke apart, both of them momentarily disorientated as though they had been beamed down from another world. Grant, for his part, was profoundly conscious his moods, attitudes and thoughts about this woman were vacillating wildly like a geiger counter exposed to radiation. She set his blood on fire, which greatly complicated their relationship. How could one think calmly, rationally when he was continually longing to make love to her? She might even see his masculine drive as excessive, a kind of male sexual aggression. She was so small, so light limbed, so fragile in his arms, the perfume of her, of her very skin, a potent trigger to desire.

By contrast she seemed shaken, deprived of speech, unusually pale.

"I'm sorry, Francesca." Remorse was in his voice. "I never meant to be rough with you. I got carried away. Forgive me. It's as you say, I lack the courtly touch."

She could have and perhaps should have told him how she felt, how she welcomed his advances with all her heart, but the tide of emotion was too dangerously high. She stood away, putting a trembling hand to her hair, realising a few long, silky strands had worked their way loose. "You didn't hurt me, Grant," she managed to say. "Appearances can be deceptive. I'm a lot tougher than I look."

His low laugh was spontaneous. "You could have fooled me." He watched her trying to fix her hair, wanting to pull it free of its braided coils. What fascination long, beautiful hair had for a man. He could even imagine himself brushing it. God he had to be mad! He forced a grin, the smile not going with the look in his eyes. "I suppose we'd better take the coffee out. It'll be getting cold." He reached around and set the glass plunger on the tray. "I'll carry it out. You relax. Get the colour back in your cheeks." A tall order when he had reduced her to a breathless quivering receptacle of sensation, naked in her clothes.

CHAPTER TWO

FRANCESCA woke with a start knowing before she even looked at the clock she had slept in. She had set the alarm for five in the morning, now it was six-ten.

"Damn!" This was too awful. She wanted to go with Grant. Francesca flung herself out of bed, glancing through the open French doors that gave onto the verandah. Sun-up four-thirty. The sky was now a bright blue, the air redolent with the wonderful smell of heat. She had even missed the morning symphony of birds, the combined voices so powerful, so swelling they regularly woke her at dawn. Sometimes the kookaburras started up their unique cackling din in predawn and she was awake to hear them, lying in bed enjoying their laughter. But she had slept deeply, exhausted by the chaos of emotion that was in her.

Still she planned to go with Grant and he'd agreed, if somewhat reluctantly. Grant had told them all before retiring he intended to wait an hour for a message to be relayed in from Bunnerong. All stations operated from dawn. Perhaps his pilot had already called in or Bunnerong had notified Kimbara of his arrival? That was the way they did it in the bush.

Hastily she splashed her face with cold water to wake herself up, cleaned her teeth and dressed in the clothes she had laid out the night before to save time. Cotton shirt, cotton jeans, sneakers. She put the brush through her hair, caught up a scarf to tie it back and rushed out into the silent hallway, padding along it until she reached the central staircase. She was almost at the bottom, when Brod came through the front door, surprise on his handsome face. "Fran? We thought we'd better let you sleep in."

Dismay hit her and she sent him a sparkling glance. "You don't mean to tell me Grant has gone without me?" Her emotions were so close to the surface she felt betrayed.

"I think he *intends* to go without you," Brod admitted wryly. "He has the firm idea you're not really up to it. Bunnerong has called in, as expected. Curly still hasn't arrived. Grant has delayed taking off for as long as he can. He's down at the airstrip refuelling."

"So he hasn't taken off yet?" Hope flashed in her eyes.

"No." Brod heaved a sigh, beginning to think Grant was right not to take her. This was his little cousin from England. He valued her highly but she wasn't used to confronting potentially dangerous situations. With no makeup and her long hair floating all around her, her cheeks pink with indignation she looked little more than a child.

"Get me down there," she said, racing towards him and taking him firmly by the arm. Literally a fire head.

Brod resisted momentarily, even though his expression was affectionate and understanding. "Fran, think about this. There's a possibility the pilot has come to some harm. That could be very distressing for you. Believe me, I *know*."

She looked up at him with her flower-blue eyes. "I won't screw up, Brod, I promise. I want to be of help. I completed a first-aid course."

Brod gave a sigh and ran his hand through his raven hair. "I don't want to be alarmist but out here accidents aren't something that happen to other people, Fran. We don't read about it in the newspapers or see it on television. They happen to *us*. All the time. Curly might be beyond first-aid. Think of that. No matter how game you are, how much you want to help, you've led a protected life.''

''Most people do. But I'm ready to *learn,* Brod.'' Francesca caught his stare and held it. ''Stop treating me like a pampered little girl. I've had my tough times as well. Now, get in and drive.'' She ran to the waiting Jeep ahead of him, almost dancing in her desire to get down to the airstrip. ''Grant promised he'd take me,'' she called over her shoulder. ''I know it mightn't be good but I'm not going to cave in. I'm half Kinross.''

She was, too, he thought with some admiration. Used as a buffer between warring parents. ''It sounds to me like you have something to prove, love,'' Brod said as he started the engine.

''Yes, I have.'' The great thing about her cousins, Brod and Ally, was they wanted to listen.

''To Grant?'' He looked at her with his all-seeing eyes, encouraging her.

''Who else?'' she flashed him her smile.

Brod nodded, his expression wry. ''He's a helluva guy, Fran, a genuinely exciting personality. He'll go far, but he's very stubborn. Once he makes up his mind you won't change it. Princess that you are you won't wind him around your little finger so be warned. Grant has very strong views. A quick pride. Strength and energy to burn. But he has lots to learn like the rest of us. We know he's deeply attracted to you but you could get hurt. Rebecca and I don't want to see that because we care about you too much.''

Francesca's delicately arching brows drew together.

"I know and I love you for it but I have to take my own chances in life, Brod. Make all my own mistakes. That's as it should be. My friendship with Grant *has* gone a step further. Everyone is aware of it. We're more involved and as a consequence we're coming increasingly into conflict."

"You know what they say. Life isn't meant to be easy. I can see it happening, Fran." Brod accelerated away from the compound. "Grant has never felt a woman's power. He's had casual affairs but they never burned him. What happens when you go back to Sydney? Have you thought of that?"

"Of course I have!" Francesca exclaimed, trying to push the thought away. "I don't want this time with you and Rebecca to end. I'm longing to see Ally when she gets home. Rafe, too, though I know he has reservations about my friendship with his 'little brother.'"

Brod chose his words carefully, knowing what she said was quite true. "Responsibility is Rafe's middle name, Fran. He damned near had to father Grant when their parents were killed. In his shock and grief Grant went more than a little wild. He was always getting into trouble, always trying to bring some daredevil prank off. That tragedy has shaped him. Put fear in him. Showed him about loss. It might well be to remember it. Grant mightn't let a woman get too close to him. His grief at the loss of his parents was enormous. He was very close to his mother as the youngest.

"They were wonderful people, the Camerons. They took pity on Ally and me and our chaotic home life. They as good as fostered us. Rafe is as close to me as a brother. Come to that I always thought of Grant as a younger brother. To love is to lose. Grant learned that early."

When they arrived at the airstrip Grant was close to taking off. He saw them coming and jumped down again onto the tarmac. There was Francesca looking like someone who should be scattering rose petals at a wedding, Titian hair flying all around her lovely head. He tried to keep a sudden anger down, wondering why he was feeling so angry at all. He didn't want her hurt. That was it. He didn't want her exposed to danger. In short he didn't want her to come.

She was running towards him, crying out in reproach. "You surely weren't going to leave without me?"

He nodded more curtly than he intended. "I don't have a real good feeling about this, Francesca. It might be better if you stay home."

"But you promised me last night." Her churning emotions sounded in her voice.

"You agree with me don't you, Brod?" Grant shot his friend a near imploring glance.

Brod considered a while. "I figure she'll come to no harm with you, Grant. She may see something she's not prepared for but knowing her I'd say she is adult enough to handle it. There may not be much wrong at all. A choke in the fuel pipe, or running too low on petrol to reach the scheduled landing."

"Which places him fair and square in a difficult and potentially dangerous situation," Grant said, feeling the pressure. "The sun is generating a lot of heat." Both men knew a lost man could dehydrate and die within forty-eight hours in the excessively dry atmosphere.

"We're all praying, Grant," Brod said.

"I know." There was tremendous mateship in the bush. Grant turned to see Francesca tying her hair back with a blue scarf for all the world as if she was donning a nurse's cap. She looked achingly young. Adolescent. No make-up. She didn't need it. No lipstick, her soft, cushiony mouth had its own natural colour. What was he to do with this magical creature? But she was game.

A few minutes later they were airborne, heading in the direction of Curly's flight path. Grant pointed to various landmarks along the way, their flight level low enough for Francesca to marvel at the primeval beauty of the timeless land.

Beneath them was lightly timbered cattle country, with sections of Kimbara's mighty herd. Silver glinted off the interlocking system of watercourses that gave the Channel Country its name. Arrows of green in the rust-red plains. Monolithic rocks of vivid orange stone thrust up from the desert floor, thickly embroidered with the burnt gold of the spinifex. The aerial view was fantastic.

Kimbara stockmen quenching their thirst with billy tea waved from the shade of the red river gums along a crescent-shaped billabong. This was vast territory. Francesca could well see how a man could be lost forever.

While Grant spoke to Bob Carlton on Opal, Francesca looked away to a distant oasis of waterholes supporting a lot of greenery in the otherwise stark desert landscape. The sky was a brilliant cloudless enamelled blue and the heat was beginning to affect her.

This wasn't the super aeroplane, the great jet she was used to on her long hauls from London to Sydney. This was a single rotor helicopter she knew little about except it could fly straight up or straight down, forwards, backwards, hover in one spot, or turn completely around. It could do jobs no other vehicle of any kind could do like land in a small clearing or on a flat roof. In many ways, a helicopter was pretty much like a magic carpet and Grant was known as a brilliant pilot. That gave her a great deal of confidence.

A lot of time passed and they saw nothing to indicate closer inspection. Francesca's eyes were moving constantly, trying not to concentrate on the extraordinary surrealistic beauty of the great wilderness, but on spotting a yellow helicopter. Huge flocks of budgerigar, the phenomenon of the outback often passed beneath them, the sunlight striking a rich emerald from their wings. She could see wild camels moving across the red sand beneath them and looking east a great outcrop of huge seemingly perfect round boulders for all the world like an ancient god's marbles.

They were now within the boundaries of Bunnerong with several large lagoons coming up. Fifteen minutes on, Grant pointed downwards then proceeded to tilt the rotary wings in that direction.

They both spotted the company helicopter at the same time. It had come to rest on a small claypan that was probably baked so hard it was like cement and virtually waterproof. Dead trees supporting colonies of white corellas like a million flowers ringed the shallow depression. A short distance off was one of the loveliest of all desert plants the casuarina, a mature desert oak with its foliage spreading out to form a graceful canopy. Beneath the oak Francesca could plainly see the body of a prone man, his face covered by the broad brim of his hat. He didn't rise at the sound of the helicopter. He didn't lift the hat away from his face. He didn't wave. He kept on lying there like a man dead.

Dear God! Francesca felt a moment of sheer terror. She had never seen death before.

In a very short time they were down on the fairly light landing pad, Grant on the radio again to let Bob Carlton back on Opal know he'd found Curly grounded, the helicopter apparently safe. More news would follow.

Outside the helicopter Francesca looked to Grant for instructions.

"Stay here," he ordered, just as she knew he would. "And take this and put it on." He handed her his akubra knowing it was much too big but it would have to do. "You go nowhere without a hat. Nowhere. And you the redhead!"

She took the reprimand meekly because she knew she deserved it. If she hadn't slept in she would have brought one of her wide-brimmed akubras. "Do what I say now," Grant further cautioned. "Stay put until I see what's going on."

It seemed sensible to obey. The birds outraged by the descent of the helicopter into their peaceful territory were wheeling in the sky, screeching a deafening protest before flying off.

She looked at Grant's broad back as he moved off, sharply aware he felt deeply responsible for this pilot. The moment he called back to her, "He's alive!" was to stay bright in Francesca's memory. She ran without thinking towards them, even though he stood up abruptly, holding up his hand.

She hadn't seen the blood. It had dried very dark, almost dyeing the pilot's shirt.

"What's happened. What is it?" she asked in considerable alarm.

"I don't know. It looks like something has attacked him." Grant strode off to the helicopter, returning with a rifle just in case. Wild boars. Bound to be plenty about. Dingo attack. He didn't think so. Then what? God forbid the attack was human. "Poor old fella! Poor Curly!" he found himself saying.

Francesca went to the unconscious man and fell to her knees. "He needs attention quite urgently. Whatever's done this to him?" Very gingerly she began to unbutton the pilot's blood-soaked shirt and as she did so he started to moan, beginning to come around.

"Here, let me take a look," Grant said urgently, gazing down at the fallen man with perplexity. "He landed the chopper quite okay. He must have become ill. Maybe he's had a heart attack. But those wounds!" Grant looked closer as Francesca working deftly peeled the shirt away. "God!" Grant exclaimed, "It's like claw marks. Feral cats."

"Could they do so much damage?" Francesca asked dubiously, used to the adorable home variety.

"They could slash you to pieces," Grant said grimly. "So many introduced animals do terrible damage to native wildlife and habitats. The camels, brumbies, foxes, wild pigs, rabbits, you name them. I've seen a man gutted by a wild boar. Feral cats aren't like your domestic tabbies. They're ferocious. More like miniature lions."

"They must be if they've done this." Francesca turned her head briefly. "Why don't you get the kit from the chopper," she urged. "I'm okay here. These wounds need to be cleaned. A lot of them seem to be fairly superficial although he's bled a great deal. Others are deep."

"They could start bleeding again," Grant warned, looking at her closely. In the shade of the casuarina she had discarded his hat, which in any case had fallen down over her eyes. She had gone very pale but her hands were rock steady.

"I'll be very careful," she said. "Blood is horrible but I won't faint if that's what's bothering you." In fact she was willing herself to remain in control. "Hello there," she said in gentle amazement as Curly opened his eyes. "Lie there quietly," she bid him swiftly, fearful his wounds would reopen. "You're fine. Fine."

Curly's alarmingly grey face took on the faintest colour. "Have I died and gone to heaven?" His voice was little more than a rusty croak.

Grant moved so he was in Curly's sights. "Hi there, Curly. I'm not paying you to rest easy under a tree."

This time Curly tried a smile. "Hi, boss. I wondered when you'd get here."

"Don't try to speak, Curly. Save your strength," Grant urged, perturbed his man looked terrible. He'd get onto the flying doctor right away. Curly could be airlifted to Bunnerong, which had its own airstrip. The Royal Flying Doctor's Cessna could land there.

"Bloody cats, would you believe it," Curly groaned. "Bloody feral cats, savage little bastards. A whole pack of them came at me out of nowhere while I was off balance being as sick as a dog. Never had such a thing happen to me before. Must have scared them somehow. Reckon I passed a kidney stone I was in so much pain. The radio is out. Needs an expert. I had to land. Just made it before I passed out. Agony I tell ya! Hell wouldn't be too strong a word for it. Now I open my eyes to an angel with eyes like the sky and hair like the sunset."

"Don't talk, Curly." Francesca smiled, knowing it was taking too much out of him. "You've had a very bad experience. I'll try not to hurt you but those scratches need attention.''

Curly gave the ghost of a cheeky grin. ''Whatever you do to me, I'll love it.''

Come to think of it she could pass for a celestial creature, Grant thought as he walked back to the helicopter to put through his calls. She could be counted on, too, to keep her head in an emergency as well. He had to admit he was impressed with her quiet efficiency.

A day later Curly was sleeping peacefully in hospital minus his gall bladder, lamenting the fact the ''angel'' who had tended his lacerations so tenderly had been replaced by a burly male nurse.

The following week saw the return of Fee and David Westbury, arms full of presents, looking wonderfully rested and increasingly affectionate after a fortnight on a small exclusive Great Barrier Reef island. Both wore becoming golden tans, Fee telling all and sundry she wasn't in the least afraid of the sun, it was ''absolutely'' essential. Of course Fee was blessed with a good olive skin, well hydrated, well cared for and she'd spent nearly all of her adult life in misty England.

''I'm not like you, my darling!'' She looked across worriedly at Francesca. ''You've got to watch yourself with that red hair and de Lyle skin. You'd shrivel up if you lived out here,'' she said innocently.

Well thank you, Mamma, Francesca heaved a small inner sigh. Thank you for confirming Grant's worst fears.

They were all at dinner in Kimbara's truly beautiful formal dining room, Brod, their host at the head of the long, gleaming mahogany table, Rebecca in a lovely aquamarine silk shift with a slightly ruffled hemline facing him at the opposite end. Fee, with David beside her was to Brod's right, ever glamorous in some kind of sophisticated tiger stripe drapery with a deep cowl neck. Facing them Francesca wore a simple shift dress similar in style to Rebecca's but a glowing midnight-blue, with Grant beside her. Their bright colouring was startling under the light from twin chandeliers. Francesca all rosy apricot reds and golds, individual strands of hair glittering like jewellery, Grant tawny bronze, hair and skin.

Brod, sensing Francesca's discomfit, and aware of Grant's misgivings about her, decided to weigh in. "Fee's just having fun, Fran," he told her lightly. "It's simply a question of taking care. Rebecca has perfect skin." Brod raised his wineglass to his beautiful wife in salute, his eyes full of admiration.

"Of course she has, darling." Fee reached out to pat his hand. "But it's that thick, creamy magnolia skin. My darling girl's is eggshell thin."

"Does that mean it can't wait to crack?" Francesca gave a little wail, her cheeks catching colour as they always did when she was upset. "Anyway eggshell may be delicate, but it's *strong*."

"The answer is as Brod says," Rebecca intervened gently. "Good sun protection and protective clothing plus the essential, wide-brimmed hat. I think Fran could not only survive but flourish out here," she added, earning Francesca's gratitude.

"Becky, darling." Fee finished her wine with amazing speed and no apparent effect. "Don't give Francesca any ideas. She's all but promised to Jimmy Waddington. That's the Honourable James Waddington. His father Peregrine is de Lyle's closest friend. Jimmy was distraught when Francesca quit her job to come to Oz. He's fully expecting her to return. As is her father. Believe me I know my daughter loves it here, but England is her real world."

"What a pity nobody told me." Francesca tried to smile, wishing for the ten thousandth time her mother wouldn't volunteer so much information. But then no one could stop Fee. She had a terrible habit of letting the cat out of the bag and if that didn't go off too well to shove it back in.

"Just knew she'd left a boyfriend behind." Grant turned his head to give Francesca a direct look. "Jimmy Waddington. The Honourable James Waddington. That sounds just about right."

"Breach of privacy, Fee." Brod tapped his aunt's magnificently beringed hand. "Now let's hear Fran's version."

Oh, thank you, Brod, Francesca thought, diving into an explanation. "I think of Jimmy as my friend. I've known him all my life. I love him in that way because he's a truly lovable person. He's decent and kind and he's very intelligent."

"In short someone you ought to marry," Grant inserted in a voice like dark polished silk.

"Except I don't love him in any romantic way. I forgot to mention that." Francesca returned his gemhard gaze.

"Believe me, darling, liking is much better." Fee of the fantastic love affairs pronounced without turning a hair. "You simply must have things in common. Have the same friends, share the same tastes, the same background. Passion is all very well but unless a man and a woman have similar views of life, things can become very quickly unstuck. Your father for instance was madly in love with me but he should never have married me.''

"I can't imagine why he did." Brod gave a brief laugh. "Obviously you were much too hard to resist, Fee, let alone control."

"Well, as they say, it seemed like a good idea at the time," Fee replied. "I desperately want my girl to be happy. I don't want her to make an awful mistake, like me. One should approach marriage in a cool and rational manner."

"That's why you did just the opposite," Francesca pointed out with less than her usual tolerance, causing David to chuckle out loud.

"Fee often says things she doesn't mean," he told Francesca soothingly. "Being in love is the grandest feeling of all. It makes one come alive. It makes one whole. Which brings me to my announcement of this evening." David tapped his crystal wineglass with a spoon and looked around the table. "Fee and I have something to tell you and we hope you'll be as happy about it as we are. We have decided to get married."

Brod was the first to respond, "Now why doesn't that surprise me?" Then everyone stood up at once. Francesca running around the table to kiss her mother, followed by Rebecca, while the men shook hands.

"Congratulations!"

"We're both so happy." A very becoming blush spread over Fee's golden cheeks. "Life is wonderful with David around. Of course he's the man I should have married."

Brod, catching David's eyes gave a sardonic little grin, but didn't point out David was married at the time. "I think this calls for champagne." He looked to his wife, loving her madly, this woman who was making him extraordinarily happy. "Would it be too much to hope we've got something really good in the frig?"

"If you're into Bollinger." She smiled into his eyes. "Some little instinct told me to put it in."

Afterwards Francesca and Grant chose to walk off the effects of the celebration, leaving Fee to talk further about her plans. The air was filled with all the clean, dry aromatic scents of the bush, the purplish black sky palpitating with the glittering white fire of countless stars. It should have been exciting but there was a kind of estrangement between them.

"So is marriage going to interfere with this movie part Fee's been offered?" Grant asked, more to break the awkward silence than anything else.

"I'm sure Mamma and David have talked it through," Francesca said. "It's not a big role. A cameo they call it. Mamma's thinking of it as a last hurrah."

"Her swan song?" Grant's deep voice sounded sceptical.

"God knows she has enormous energy and a great deal to offer. Anyway David's used to Mamma," Francesca said. "She's right about one thing. They're two of a kind. David has always led a full life, a pivotal member of a very glamorous group, the theatre, the art aficionados. He's very different from Daddy. My father likes the companionship of a few lifelong friends and his own peaceful world of Ormond. He hates leaving it even for a day."

"I expect it's very beautiful."

"One of the most beautiful places on earth." Francesca felt her heart swelling with pride.

"But you won't inherit it?" Grant countered with a kind of disbelief.

Francesca plucked a waxy flower then twirled it under her nose. "No."

"Good Lord!" Grant stared up at the pulsing stars. "Don't you mind, this male of the line stuff?"

"Perhaps." She nodded, in reality deeply attached to her ancestral home. "But I grew up knowing I wouldn't inherit Ormond, just as Ally knew Kimbara would be Brod's."

"A bit of a difference there, I'd say." Grant sounded as if he didn't appreciate the parallel. "The business of running a cattle chain is all hard slog. Backbreaking work, stoic resilience, lots of responsibility. I wouldn't wish the load on any woman's shoulders. The outback is a man's world, Francesca, for all we need our women's love and devotion. You would be in perfect harmony with your ancestral home."

She'd been counting on him to say that. "Only it's *not* mine," she repeated wryly. Hadn't she already moved out, not at all close to her father's second wife, not able to help making comparisons with a beautiful, brilliant Fee.

"That's too damned bad," Grant was saying. "If I were your father I'd have changed things."

"I'm very glad you're not my father," she offered dryly, deeply conscious of his tall, powerful figure beside her, whipcord lean.

He laughed, then suddenly began to croon, taking her by surprise. "You must have been a beautiful baby. You must have been a beautiful child. When you were only startin' to go to kindergarten, I bet you drove the little boys wild...."

Perfect tune. Smooth as honey baritone. It sounded great with a considerable degree of seductiveness.

"I didn't know you could sing," she said delight-edly.

"Of course I can sing." The ice broken he pulled her against him, wrapping an arm around her waist. "You should hear me when I'm out riding. When I was a kid I used to sing to the cattle. It used to calm them every time."

"Are you serious?" she laughed.

"Ask Rafe." He launched smoothly into another song. "Home, home on the range…"

His voice came back to them on the wind and Francesca clapped in appreciation. "From now on you're going to have to serenade *me*."

"Am I?" He turned her, his hands spanning her nar-row waist. "So what about this Jimmy?"

She dipped her head. "Daddy's choice, Grant. Not mine."

"You're not running away from them, are you?" he asked as if he were resolved to find out. Holding her, touching her, desire rippling deep inside him.

"In what way?"

"Unwillingness to commit maybe. Your father is concerned with marrying you off properly. He doesn't trust your mother in that regard."

"He doesn't trust Fee at all," Francesca confessed wryly. "He may have loved her madly once but all I can remember is his finding fault. It's not very nice being the child in the middle of a fault-finding divorce and the long aftermath. The physical separation from Mamma. It was like being deprived of the sun. The actor Fee was having an affair with and later married was remarkably handsome and when he wasn't drunk he could be very nice but Daddy *hated* him. He refused to allow me to visit if Fee's 'new man' was anywhere around.''

"Well he wasn't around long, thank the Lord." Grant gave a deep sigh. Fee's exploits over the years were well known to all of them. He had a vivid picture, too, of how it must have been for one sad and solitary little girl.

"I can give you some lyrics à la Cole Porter," Francesca offered half in fun, half serious. "'It was just one of those things. One of those crazy things.' Fee can't be without a man."

"Now she's got David, so cheer up." Grant turned her gently so they could walk on.

"And my dear cousin, David, will keep Mamma in line," Francesca said with a note of satisfaction. "He may look and act the perfect gentleman with the Eton accent but he's steel at the core. If he'd been married to Fee in the first place she'd never have shared anyone else's bed."

"Her time with your father could scarcely have been wasted," Grant reminded her. "She had *you.* That alone was a great gift. Anyway she adores you."

"I know." Forgiving by nature Francesca's anger and bewilderment at her mother's abandonment had long since dried up.

"And you're going back to Sydney for her book launch." It was obviously a statement, not a question.

"Of course I have to and I want to. Rebecca as the biographer is going as a matter of course. It's just a pity Ally won't be home. I want to be here when she gets back."

"And I need to be *out!*" Grant startled her by saying.

Anxiety sounded in her voice. "What does that mean?"

He gave a little amused growl low in his throat. "Why, Francesca, do I really have to spell it out? Two's company, three's a crowd. Especially when you're newly married."

She stood stock-still to stare up at him. "But the homestead is so big!"

"What's wrong, love?" Very lightly he pinched that delicately determined little chin. "Don't you like it? Rafe and Ally will want to be on their own."

Privately she thought Rafe and Ally would be very upset if he left. "But where will you go?" she questioned. "I never thought for a minute you'd leave Opal. Apart from the fact it's your home, it's the base for Cameron Airways."

"That can be changed." He sounded as if he'd thought it all out.

"You're serious then?" She was totally distracted.

"Absolutely."

"Do Rafe and Ally know of your plans?" she persisted, so nearly giving herself away.

"Not as yet. Needless to say they assure me Opal is my home as well."

"I should think so." Francesca felt like she was in some trance of non-acceptance. She couldn't lose contact with this man she'd fallen helplessly, probably hopelessly in love with. "Where would you go?"

Grant took her hand and walked on. "Somewhere more central. Even Darwin."

"In the Territory?" She was shaken by the thought. He was talking a thousand miles away and more.

"Gateway to Australia." Grant nodded. "I know of a fine property that could come on the market."

Francesca gave him a dismayed look, unaware her expression was easily readable by the moon. "You've taken my breath away," she told him unnecessarily. "Everyone will miss you terribly." *Me* most of all.

For a long moment he was mad with wanting her. Wanting to crush her to him, feel the softness and smallness of her body against his. Inhale her scents. Instead with force of will he pressed his thumb into her palm, feeling her heat, caressing it with a deep circular motion. What stopped him from making love to this young woman as he was wild to? Other times, other places, other girls, he had felt none of this anguish over lovemaking. The answer was he cared too damned much about her. He couldn't force a potentially disastrous situation. She was Lady Francesca de Lyle, daughter of an English earl and the internationally famous stage actress, Fiona Kinross. If she were any other girl, a young woman of his own circle, he'd have raced her to the altar. Francesca's background reeked of centuries old tradition, a high place in one of the most privileged societies on earth. Even Fee had pushed the fact Francesca was meant for better things.

Finally he managed to say, "I'm not going that far away. Not as a plane flies. I don't aim to stick to helicopters. Dad left me a fair share of Opal even if I'm not Numero Uno."

You are to me, Francesca thought, blindly turning her face away. "Why don't you build a homestead of your own on Opal?" she frowned. "There's plenty of room in a couple of thousand square miles."

His spirits lifted unaccountably. Why hadn't he come around to that? "Opal has only ever had one homestead," he pointed out as if it was written in stone.

She shot him a quick look, aware of his change of mood. "Two Cameron sons who love each other and don't want to be parted? Even if they don't want to share the same house, I would have thought building another homestead would be the obvious solution. And I'll tell you exactly where you should do it."

He was halfway to laughing now, loving the sweet sound of her voice and the surprising authority in it. "Go on. Tell me," he invited, taking the path that led to the walled garden with its pond and winged nymph, glorious scents of roses, jasmine and boronia, herbs crushed underfoot, soft little night wind like music and two carved garden seats.

Peace and harmony by day. Powerfully seductive by moonlight. Maybe he'd been worrying so much he'd suddenly got to the point where he couldn't care anymore. Whatever the reason he led her to one of the benches, sending a few fallen leaves and spent blossoms flying with a lick of the handkerchief from his trouser pocket. Protecting her pretty deep blue dress was a priority. The short skirt showed her lovely legs. The deep oval neck descended onto her breasts, delicate, tantalising, the skin of the upper slopes smooth as silk, white as milk. The rosy nipples he just knew would be like luscious little berries in his mouth, the taste more exquisite than any known fruit.

God the only thing that saved him from ravishing her was he knew right from wrong. Even so his breath seemed to be rasping in his chest. Desire was the very devil. It made an utter fool of a man.

"I would have thought you'd guess," Francesca was saying, making room for him on the bench, mercifully unaware of his unsettled state. "It's extraordinary country and it's only about a mile or more from Opal homestead. Grassy flats, bordered by spinifex and mulga country, then in the distance the rippling slopes of the desert dunes. But what makes it all fascinating is that very strange hill with the perfectly flat top, except for three little peaks around the border for all the world like some ancient crown. It's full of magic. Every time I've seen it, from the distance or the air, it seems to be floating in an amethyst mirage.''

Of course he identified the site right away. Francesca was right. There was something about it. ''Francesca, you're talking about Myora,'' he said, referring to the landmark. ''There are all kinds of legends attached to it.''

''Which makes it all that more delightful,'' she said happily. ''As hills go it isn't high. What would it be…a couple of hundred feet? But it has such an *aura!*'' Then she suddenly asked, ''It's not a sacred site?'' She knew that could change things with aboriginal tribes currently focusing on regaining their sacred sites.

''No—'' Grant shook his head, instantly following her line of thought ''—but it has associations from the Dreamtime.''

''Does that mean you can't build there?'' She felt unaccountably disappointed.

''I can build anywhere I want,'' he told her firmly. ''This is Cameron land. We feel we have as much kinship with the land as our aboriginal brothers. The Camerons have always treated tribal people well. We came as protectors as well as pastoralists. As a courtesy I would discuss my plans with the tribal elders. But, Francesca, Myora is even more isolated than Opal homestead.''

''You mean the difficulty of getting building materials, etc., to the site?'' Immediately Francesca was overwhelmed by the challenges of the job.

"No, I don't," Grant said surprisingly. "Our forebears performed fantastic feats. I mean—'' he broke off, rubbing his neck. "Hell I don't know what I mean." When every other thought was given over to placing Francesca, like a jewel, in her proper setting. The middle of the Never Never, for all its fascination, didn't seem the right spot.

"You could *think* about it," Francesca suggested, looking up at his strong profile.

"Wouldn't you be terrified on your own out there?" he countered.

Another rejection. "What should I be terrified of?" She kept her voice composed. "There aren't any bushrangers anymore. No stockman would dream of causing me harm."

"You know nothing about utter isolation," he said, leaning a little away from her. "When you come out here you stay at one of the grandest homesteads in the country. Kimbara. You're safe and cushioned at all times. I love the bush, Francesca, I have great respect for it but I can tell you even hardened stockmen can get spooked on their own. There are some areas, some places, that have an atmosphere, that can make the hair on the back of your neck stand up. We've all experienced it. This is an incredibly ancient land. We're by way of being very recent newcomers."

Francesca gave a delicious little shiver. "Are we talking ghosts?"

"I'm not talking ballyhoo, my lady," he retorted, giving a lock of her long hair a slight tug. "What I say isn't to be taken lightly. There are certain places even the aborigines won't go."

"On Opal?" She felt as if she was drowning in mysteries.

"Of course on Opal." Grant's voice was matter-of-fact. "Kimbara, too. It's *strange* country in many ways. Our country and not our country. Not the white man's country if you know what I mean. Our ancestors came from elsewhere. The Camerons and the Kinrosses hailed from Scotland. In certain places the Interior seems to be not exactly hostile but not welcoming, either."

"You can't mean Myora?" She'd always thought the land welcomed her on all her visits.

Grant's voice was level. "*I've* never felt it there. But *you've* never actually been there, have you?"

"I'd like to go." She lifted a delicate brow.

"Then this is your chance," he surprised her by answering. "I have a few days all to myself. I can take you tomorrow, though the odds are against my ever building there."

"You might change your mind." She attempted lightness when she was feeling utterly emotional.

"Wishful thinking, Francesca." He turned his hazel eyes on her.

"*What* am I thinking?" Suddenly she could barely breathe. There was humour in his voice but something else that sent a deep pulsing, quiver right through her body.

"An impossible dream."

"What dream," she challenged, softly. "What am I dreaming?"

For answer he bent his head and pressed his mouth to the creamy flesh of her throat.

"Grant!" Even to her own ears she sounded startled.

"You don't really know what you're trying to get yourself into," he said, a shade harshly.

"Can't you see you surprised me?" In fact she was more frightened of her own reactions than anything he might do to her. He was the most beautiful man. Full of a man's powers. Just the touch of his lips against her throat made her head swim.

"You're safe with me, Francesca," he said in a dry voice and stood up, his height exaggerated in the silver moonlight. "As safe as if you were sitting in church."

She, too, came to her feet, humming with tension. "Now I've made you angry, why?"

"I'm not angry with you at all," he said, not really meaning it and not knowing why. "I just don't want you to forget who *you* are and who *I* am."

"Now that's a *message*," Francesca said.

"Yes, it is." Even he grimaced, thinking himself as much a victim of circumstances as Francesca.

"Why can't you get through your head I'm a *woman* not a figurine," Francesca suddenly exploded.

That somehow inflamed him to the point he felt he was burning up. *He* didn't appreciate she was a woman? How could she say such a ridiculous thing, this miracle of femininity.

Before she could take a breath he held her lovely face and kissed her hard and fast. Just seconds to be ravenous. He wanted to plunge his hand into the low, tempting oval of her dress and take hold of her small creamy breasts. Just the thought of it made him wild, but he couldn't do this to her. It was all so damned confusing. One might have thought she was some kind of family, or a little Titian-haired, blue-eyed saint on a pedestal. He should have avoided her right from the start. She was so hopelessly out of reach.

Francesca's own confusion was immense. Grant was breathing heavily. So was she. Both of them filled with a terrible unrequited desire. More than that. Love. She was certain he loved her but instead of helping her it was somehow making him feel guilty. She could have wept.

"Grant, I really care about you," she said, moving close, gripping onto his shirtsleeve with her hand. "Why are you pushing me away?"

"You know very well." That high mettled note came into his voice. "I care about you, too, Francesca. Too much to want to cause you real unhappiness. I can see to the end of this if you can't?"

It was obvious his concerns were real. "You mean you think it inevitable I'll go back to England."

"You'll leave me before I'll ever leave you. England *is* your home. You have a certain position in life. It's not outback wife. Even the heat of the sun can be killing."

She was nearly crying with frustration. "So Rebecca can survive it. So can Ally, so can my mother. Every other woman it seems but me."

He looked down at her, she was totally enchanting and anguish edged his voice. "It's the way you look."

"You think I'm an ice cream that might melt." She made a little sound of exasperation.

"Hell I'm afraid of just that. Look, Francesca, I'm not trying to insult you—" he stroked her cheek "—or anything like that. I'm trying to decide what's best for both of us."

"Which of course is as good as saying *I'm* stupid." She shimmered with sudden temper.

"Far from it." He knew he shouldn't but he laughed, loving the sparkle in her star-struck eyes.

"Then why don't you let me decide what *I* want," she challenged, her blue gaze riveted to his strong handsome face.

"Because it's too dangerous." He bent his head and just brushed the corner of her mouth with his lips. "You're hell bent on a holiday romance."

She heard the teasing note in his voice…of course she did, yet she flinched. "Then it's really astonishing the way *you* keep kissing *me*."

He grinned at her, his teeth flashing very white. "That's what's called turning the tables. I'm sorry, Francesca, you might have started up the saying, you're adorable when you're angry, but I don't want to hurt you. You make me feel as protective as a big brother."

"Oh Lord!" She inhaled the jasmine-boronia filled night air. "So we don't get to take our trip tomorrow?"

He smiled slightly. "Hell you can't go around disappointing me. Of course we will. I wouldn't forego it for the world. You're going to show me where to build my dream house."

"Why should I?" she questioned, turning up her face to him. Why? When he would take to it some other woman as his bride.

"Because you're Lady Francesca de Lyle," he explained in a voice like dark velvet. "And it's your gift to me."

CHAPTER THREE

"YOU'RE going to do what?" Fee burst out, turning from the French doors and walking back into Francesca's bedroom.

"You heard, Mamma," Francesca continued, brushing her hair at the mirror. It was crackling with electricity, red, amber, rose and gold strands sparkling and flashing. "I'm going over to Opal with Grant. I'm going to help him pick out a home site."

"I don't believe it." Fee's dramatic face wore a worried frown. She slumped into a comfortable armchair imagining she was having a nervous breakdown. "I must ask you darling, is this wise?"

"Of course it's wise, Mamma," Francesca responded respectfully, firmly.

"But you know, darling, your father has big plans for you," Fee reminded her. "I might have embodied his biggest nightmare but you're his dream child. He loves you. He wants to see you happy in your own setting. Married to one of your childhood friends."

"Like good old Jimmy, my ex-boyfriend," Francesca asked wryly, waiting for her hair to settle so she could braid it.

"Not Jimmy if you don't think you could come to love him," Fee told her, reasonably. "But there are others, darling. Roger and Sebastian to name just two."

"Except I don't love them, either. Daddy didn't ask my permission to marry Holly. He just mentioned to me he was thinking of remarrying."

62

"How extraordinary when he hated every minute of being married to me," Fee said, gazing at her lovely daughter tenderly, maternally.

"No, he didn't, Mamma," Francesca corrected, ever loyal to her father. "He loved you. He would have stayed married to you forever if you hadn't run off."

"It must have been Springtime," Fee said, her face reflective. "Actually I was terribly misled but I was always hotly desired."

"You won't run away from David," Francesca warned.

"Darling, as if I'd want to!" Fee protested going quite pink. "At long last I've got it right. Best thing I've ever done. Anyway it's not me we're talking about, it's you. Don't think for a minute I have anything against Grant. He's a splendid young man, so sexy, he even gives your dear Mamma a funny feeling, but he has his own vision in life. Why only last night he was telling us his plans. His commitment is *here*. The Australian outback."

"Don't you think you're running too far ahead?" Francesca said, making little braids of her front hair.

Fee snorted. "Come on, darling, I know everything there is to know about love affairs. The air literally crackles around you two."

"Holiday affair?" Francesca asked.

"Well if you have to get him out of your system," Fee considered. "I don't see you two together, my darling. I can only see heartache and separation. I know it's not easy but one must try to be wise."

Francesca raised a delicate brow. "Yes, of course, Mamma, but I'm only going over to help him pick out a possible site for a new homestead. Grant doesn't want to intrude on Rafe and Ally."

"Goodness how nice of him," Fee said. "But the place is *huge*. Besides, why couldn't he buy a property? Douglas would have left his sons very well provided for."

"I'm certain Rafe doesn't want to lose his brother," Francesca said. "They're very close. Closer than most because of the sad circumstances of their life. Why buy another property when Grant could build a second homestead on Opal. Lord knows they've got a whole world to themselves as Brod has here."

"A kingdom at the very least," Fee agreed complacently. "My friends used to find it fascinating listening to stories from my childhood on Kimbara. But don't try to distract me. I'm doing my best to play Mamma. In short, I'm trying to warn you, my darling. You could get badly hurt. So could Grant. I should tell you, too, the Camerons are men of strong passions. And proud. Fiercely proud. You'll have to live with that."

"Actually I like it," Francesca said, her eyes going dreamy.

Fee fell back, unable to keep the genuine worry out of her voice. "Darling, normally I wouldn't interfere but I have a feeling this could be very serious. What have you really got on your mind? Surely as your mother I'm entitled to know?"

Francesca found herself sinking into the armchair opposite her mother. "I've never felt like this before, Mamma," she explained. "I feel like I'm lit up inside."

"You're in love." Fee nodded. "It's just rotten luck you had to fall for Grant."

Instantly Francesca jumped up, outraged. "That's not funny, Mamma."

Fee, too, hauled herself to her feet. "I'm not trying

to be funny, darling. For heaven's sake! I'm worried where this might lead. You have *everything* at home in England.''

''Except Grant,'' Francesca said with a touch of fire.

''Maybe so.'' Fee started to sound doubtful. ''But this life couldn't be more *different*, Fran. You've never seen Kimbara under drought. In times of flood. You can't possibly know. You haven't been around when the tragedies happen. Let's face it, darling, do you really want this lifestyle? Can you cope with it?''

''Rebecca is blooming,'' Francesca told her.

''Rebecca isn't *you* and I expect she'll take up her writing again. She'll have something engrossing to do. She and Brod will start a family. Kimbara needs its heirs.''

''What about Ally then?'' Francesca challenged, feeling like everyone was against her. ''Ally could have had a huge movie career. She knocked it all back for Rafe.''

''Oh, darling.'' Fee returned to her chair looking at her daughter with pity in her eyes. ''Ally is that little bit older than you, and she's had longer to consider what she really wants out of life. Then there's the fact, good actress that she is, Ally wasn't really dedicated as one has to be. The theatre was *everything* to me. That's the difference.'' But there had been a devastation to it, Francesca thought, but was too tender-hearted to mention. Her mother had been a wonderful actress but she hadn't been the best of mothers.

''A career isn't the only way to happiness and fulfilment, Mamma,'' she said quietly, sitting on the edge of the four-poster bed. ''It's a big job raising a family and I want children. I'd rather find Mr. Right than be a huge success in the business world though most people would tell you I was very effective at P.R.''

"And it didn't hurt to have an earl for a father," Fee pointed out dryly.

"That doesn't give me a warm glow, Mamma." Francesca couldn't help but speak a little sharply. "In many ways your view of me seems to be as a *child.*"

It was true. "Ah well, you are very young, darling," Fee sighed. "Moreover you're the bearer of your father's dream. You're bright, beautiful, charming, so clearly destined for big things. You must realise, too, your son could become your father's heir."

Francesca looked at her mother levelly. "Even Grant has pointed that out to me."

Fee nodded. "I'm sure it concerns him. Whatever his feelings for you he must be aware of the situation."

"*What* situation," Francesca burst out in pure frustration. "Anyone would think I was a member of the Royal Family. Grant and I are equals. Come to that you always had more money than Daddy. I know you helped extensively at Ormond."

"You can say that again!" Fee breathed. "But I don't feel at all bitter about it. It's as I say, one day my grandson might occupy it. I don't want to be disagreeable, darling. I don't want to upset you. I know the wonderful feelings that come with thinking oneself in love but I have to help you to look steadily to your future. I feel a great affection for the Camerons, Rafe and Grant. Grant is an admirable young man. There's no question he's going places. He's masterful, aggressive, assertive and very hot-headed from time to time. You may find it exciting now but as he develops I think he'll turn into a real dynamo. Dynamos in a way are dangerous people. They're high risk."

"I'm not afraid of anything about Grant, Mamma," Francesca said very seriously, twining her arms around the polished mahogany bedpost, all rose and cream and blue sheened eyes. "I think he'd die rather than hurt me. What makes me fearful is the thought he could turn me away thinking it was for my own good."

Fee gave an uncomfortable little laugh. "Darling, have you considered he might be right?" Breeding showed in every line of her daughter's petite, slender body, breeding and what Fee interpreted as a certain fragility, an inability to withstand rigours.

Her mother's seeming opposition was like little barbs to the heart. Francesca moved off the bed so quickly her thick braid swung against her cheek. "Except if I lost him I know I'd be sorry for the rest of my life."

They landed on Opal's front lawn while the hot humming earth sent up spirals of dried grass, bleached bronze and gold leaves. When the air was still they alighted, Francesca looking with great pleasure towards the huge, rambling old homestead with its gables and verandah bays, the pedimented porch and the white wrought-iron lacework that matched the timber fretwork. Opal lacked Kimbara's conscious grandeur but it was a fine colonial homestead by anyone's standards. Cascading bright red bougainvillea made a glorious show falling from the slate roof of the east wing, down the white pillars to the ground, as did the deep hardy border of agapanthus with huge hyacinth and white heads right along the front of the house, but it was evident not a great deal of time had been spent on the once extensive home gardens. The lawn not shaded by a giant magnolia and a row of classic gums, was yel-

lowed by the heat of the sun and the central three tiered
fountain that once had played was now dry and dusty.
Nevertheless it was an amazingly attractive building
and Francesca knew Ally would have the most wonderful time bringing the homestead and its home
grounds back to their former glory.

"Come up and look around," Grant said, taking her
by her silky arm, feeling the sizzle in his fingers. "It's
very quiet with no one around. As you can see, the
gardens of my mother's day have gone, neither Rafe
nor I have had the time to look after them. Not that
either of us know much about gardening but we surely
miss what it was like with Mum around. That wonderful feminine grace went out of everything. But Ally
will bring it back."

Francesca looked up to smile into his face, feeling
so happy it was like her blood was filled with bubbles.
"And have a marvellous time doing it. I *love* the homestead." Her eyes shone. "It's extraordinarily pictur-
esque. As a matter of fact now I look at it, it would be
the ideal outback setting for Mamma's new movie?"

"What are you saying here?" Grant cocked a brow.
"I thought the woman director was coming out to take
a look at Kimbara? Surely Fee said so at dinner last
night?"

"Actually, Mamma did that without asking,"
Francesca confessed. "Something she has a tendency
to do. Not that Brod would refuse her and Rebecca
would take pleasure in it but I've read the screenplay
and Kimbara homestead is too…too…" She sought the
right word.

"Teetering on grand?" he suggested dryly.

"In every way. Uncle Stewart spent a fortune on its
upkeep and it shows."

"While the Camerons did not." He looked her straight in the eyes, loving her sudden flush, a rosy pinkness that wasn't there a moment ago.

"I don't mean that." Francesca shook her head. "I mean Opal has a soft well lived in…"

"Faded charm?"

"Are you going to finish all my sentences for me?" she demanded.

"If we want to get to the nitty gritty." He grinned, moving her into the shade of the verandah.

"If you read the screenplay you'd know what I mean."

"Francesca, I'm one up on you." His smile mocked her. "I've read the book."

"*Have* you?" She sounded delighted.

"Outback people are great readers," he told her. "Didn't you know?"

"As a matter of fact I do." Reading was a big part of entertainment. "Opal homestead is really what they're after."

"Maybe, but who would need all those film people around?" He opened the front door, turning to look at her in her simple cotton shirt and jeans. Who said a redhead couldn't wear pink? He'd never seen a pink shirt look so good.

"You said yourself it was very lonely on your own." Her eyes were alive with ideas. "I expect the outback scenes could be shot in a month. Riversleigh, the Sydney colonial mansion is the setting for most of the action. Anyway it's just a thought."

"Then why are those blue eyes so bright and alive?" he retorted with amusement. "The last time they sparkled just like that you were doing an excellent P.R. job on Drew Forsythe from TCR."

"I'm always full of ideas," Francesca said, moving into the spacious hallway and looking around.

"I can see that," he commented, captivated by her presence.

"So am I allowed to discuss it with Mamma?" She twirled her small supple body. "The director and script writer will be here in a couple of days."

"You're kidding?" In a way he was utterly taken aback.

"No," she answered simply. "It would be lovely to see Opal up on the big screen. It's not the first time a colonial mansion has been used in an Australian movie. I think it would be brilliant! Moreover you have such enormous interest in everything you'd probably enjoy it."

"Well I might," he admitted, "but, Francesca, I'm not around much during the day. I have a business."

"All right. So no one would bother you. There would be good company for dinner. You would want to speak to Rafe and Ally?"

He laughed. A mocking sound, slightly awry. "Darling, are you reminding me of my obligations?"

The way he called her "darling" nearly took her breath away. "Really I'm just having a bit of fun," she wavered.

"No, you're not." The laugh turned indulgent. "You want me to take this seriously."

"I swear I never thought of it until five minutes ago," she said sincerely. "I looked up at the homestead and there it was! The setting right under my nose, so to speak."

"They pay well I imagine?" Grant the business man was considering.

"I'm sure they would."

"In that case Rafe is involved in a programme for rehabilitation for troubled youth, a kind of bush rescue scheme. I'm interested, too, but as Rafe runs the station it's mainly his concern. The Trust could do with the money."

"What a good idea." She felt a real flutter of excitement. "I've heard about the scheme from Ally. I can see, too, the bush has great healing powers.

"Nature's cathedral," Grant said. "God can speak very clearly here. But hang on, Francesca, your mother has other ideas."

"Not by the time I've spoken to her." Francesca gave her lovely endearing smile.

"I believe you, but you'll have to hang on until I speak to Rafe and Ally. They mightn't want any part of it."

Francesca lifted her face to him. "I'm not exactly sure about Rafe, but I know Ally will be intrigued. She might even want to be home when they shoot the scenes. We'll all enjoy watching Fee. She becomes so much the part she's playing, it's shivery. As soon as the makeup goes on, the dress, she's that person."

Grant could well believe it. He'd seen Fee transform herself into any number of people in the space of telling a story. "You've never thought of acting yourself?" he asked Francesca.

"Believe it or not I was considered quite good at school."

"So did Fee go along to see you? Tell you how wonderful you were?"

The smile faltered slightly. "She was so busy at the time she missed all of my performances, but Daddy came."

"Hell I put my foot in it," he groaned, so much in empathy with her he felt her old pain.

"It doesn't hurt anymore."

"Sure?" He badly wanted to kiss her, hold her in his arms, comfort her, only he was too keenly aware it could all get out of hand. She made his blood soar, this exquisitely fashioned young woman. Not a figurine. She had far too much intelligence, humour, radiance to be that.

"I don't think I could love Mamma any more than I do. I *know* she's not ordinary but I have missed her terribly many times in my life." Read years, Francesca thought but would never say. Not now when the estrangement was over.

"It could have ruined your relationship forever," Grant considered broodingly, "but you're far too compassionate for that. Fee was perfectly charming to me when we left, but I got the feeling she's afraid of something."

"Oh, Grant, don't talk about it." She came to him and took his hand, trying to distract his attention. "I feel like a cup of coffee and I want to look over the homestead."

"You know you're safe with me, don't you," he said, not to be deflected.

She stared right into his eyes. "To me you're the most honourable man on the face of the earth."

"Francesca!" He couldn't help it, he pulled her into his arms as his emotions took control. "I have to tell you I'm suffering for it." His tone was self-mocking and dry.

"What could be wrong about falling in love?" she whispered rejoicing in being within the circle of his arms.

"Falling in love is wonderful, Francesca," he agreed in a low feeling voice. "The world is a lovely, romantic place, but there's no question falling in love with the wrong person can wreck lives."

"Then why don't you let me go," she taunted him very gently, lifting her head.

His expression was wry. "It seems my arms have a life of their own."

"So you are happy to hold me?"

"I love holding you," he said and meant it. "I could hold you like this forever. I could spend eternity looking into your eyes. I could run my mouth over that little pulse in your throat. I could open that pink shirt and caress your breasts. I could topple you into my bed. But that wouldn't get the coffee made." Determinedly he bent his head, kissed her cheek and swiftly turned her about. "Do you like it black or white?"

"You're a devil," she said. So he was for tempting her so richly.

"There's a devil in every man," he warned her, his eyes glinting," but depend on it I'll keep him well hidden around you."

They took the horses along the long, twisting trail of gullies and billabongs that led to the ancient flat-topped hill the aborigines named Myora. At intervals they came across stockmen leading herds of cattle to camp, stopping briefly to watch an aboriginal stockman breaking in a silver-grey brumby obviously descended from station stock. The stockman's movements were filled with a kind of exquisite grace and Francesca was reminded Australian aborigines were among the finest natural dancers in the world. Overhead legions of birds flew like bright flags in the sky and there was music, too, from thousands and thousands of tiny throats with occasionally a wonderful cello solo from some bell-toned bird in the furthermost branch of a towering gum, or deep in the swamp.

There were kangaroos of all sizes, a marvellous sight when they bounded away across the flats, endearing standing stock-still by the water as they picked up their scent, ears pricked, pointed noses quivering, a curious look in their large, bright eyes. Through all this wonderful ride, Grant kept exclusively to the shade, following the tree-lined creeks that were scented with acacia and some kind of little lilies that grew thickly guarded by grand old coolabahs and ghost gums. At one of the many reed fringed billabongs they saw masses of waterfowl, and several times the wonderful blue cranes, the brolgas, making a striking picture as they fished among the waterlilies. Pink in this lagoon, blue in another, sometimes a mixture of blue and cream. Francesca, the nature lover, was utterly enchanted, thinking as she always did, the bush was a place of great magic. Her mother's blood truly spoke to her. She had absorbed it into her soul.

By the time they reached Myora there was a taut expectancy in the air. Because of the extreme flatness of the vast open plains even an elevation of a few hundred feet took on a considerable aura. Today as she had seen it from the air Myora's base was floating in a sea of amethyst mirage giving the impression the ancient eroded mesa was anchored to a cloud. To north, south, east and west the plains ran on for endless miles. In fruitful years wildflowers bloomed in their countless millions, way out to the far horizon but even in the Dry it was a magnificent sight.

"You're really enjoying yourself, aren't you?" Grant said with immense satisfaction, keeping a sharp look out for anything to startle her, a large goanna, a prowling dingo, the frilled lizards that came at a lightning rush but were harmless, some slight movement at the base of a bush that could only be a snake trying to escape.

"This is a special place," Francesca breathed, watching as Grant hitched the horses to a huge fallen tree limb for all the world like a massive sculpture. "This is where you should build your house. Right in the middle of the sweeping plain with Myora as a backdrop. It must be an incredible sight when the great inland blooms. I've missed it on every visit."

"You'll have to come back when the time is right," Grant managed to say in a casual voice, at the same time feeling a deep ache that took a moment or two to pass. "Flowers as far as the eye can see," he continued. "Mile after mile, the flowers go on. Over the graves of the pioneers. Over the graves of the lost explorers. The flowers are fragrant as well so the air might be blown in from heaven. Last year after the winter rains the country around here was smothered in yellow and white paper daisies, golden craspedia, green pussy tails, poppies and firebush, hopbush saltbush, yellow top carpet of snow, you name it. Though I've witnessed the flowering of the desert gardens all my life in times of drought even I can't believe the flowers will ever rise again. Yet they always do."

"A miracle," Francesca said quietly, still badly shaken by his casual acceptance she would be returning home.

He walked towards her, tall and powerful. "It sure seems like it. Experiments have been done on the remarkable desert seeds. Apparently they contain chemicals that prevent germination until the optimum time. Nature's green light. They don't spring to life for example after a brief shower only to quickly die back. The right timing ensures the seed crop for future generations." He pointed upwards to the ancient glowing hill.

"At the right times, there are beautiful blooms hidden away up there on Myora. Tucked into all sorts of places where the wind has blown the seeds. Fan flowers, wild hibiscus, little lilies, Lilac Lamb's Tails literally covering the rubble down the hillside, all waving in the breeze. Anyway, come along." He took hold of her hand. "I've something special to show you. Something we don't talk about a great deal on Opal mainly for protection."

"That's exciting! What is it?" She stared up into his golden-skinned face, his iridescent eyes shadowed by the broad brim of his akubra.

"All in good time." He stopped, touching a gentle forefinger to her chin. "God, you're beautiful!" He truly didn't mean to say it but it just popped out. Why was he sending out all these dangerous, conflicting, messages? Only her lovely face looked so rapt.

"I'm happy," she told him.

"That's what I want you to be." He spoke quietly but something in his voice turned hard. "Let's climb to the summit." He drew her on. "It's not that far and it's amazing the view of the surrounding countryside.

Despite his contradictions, a not to be denied exhilaration took hold of Francesca. It lent wings to her small feet. She was like a gazelle going up the rocky slope, foot sure, keeping hold of his hand but making her own confident ascent.

"Oh, this is marvellous!" she announced, when they finally reached the plateau.

"Get your breath," he advised, knowing he was being overprotective.

"I'm not out of breath." She showed a radiant smile to him.

"No, you're not," he admitted.

"It's all so vast!" She turned away from him and threw up her arms. "Overwhelming. I love the colours of the inland. All the ochres. They're so deep and weathered yet they *vibrate*. And the sky's so blue. Not a cloud in sight. The European explorers must have thought they'd ventured onto another planet. Thousands of square miles with not a soul in it except for nomadic tribes. And that sea of red sand dunes on the horizon sweeping on and on forever."

He went to her and checked her progress towards the rim. "Deserts are powerful landscapes. They're also death traps, so don't forget it. Knowledge is the thing. Modern transport, equipment. Even then things go wrong."

"Hey, Grant, you can't put me off," she warned gently.

"I can see that."

"Besides the Channel Country is a riverine desert," she pointed out. "All this wonderful network of interlocking rivers and creeks. The billabongs and lagoons."

"In drought except for the permanent billabongs they go dry," Grant told her. "In flood the rivers run for miles across. That's what the Channel Country *is*, a vast flooded plain. It covers a good five percent of the continent. During the monsoonal months the deserts to the north and here can be hit by fierce electrical storms. One claimed Stewart Kinross's life. Almost claimed Rebecca's. The roars of thunder are quite terrifying and they're accompanied by tremendous flashes of lightning. When lightning hits the inflammable spinifex we can have grass fires for days.''

''So you're telling me it's a beautiful savage land.''

''One has to remember that at all times.''

''Yet it's so incredibly peaceful.'' Francesca looked out over the endless open vista. ''Man needs the wilderness. These vast, open plains. There's such dignity about the outback. So much character. When one loves city life, cities are the place to be. I've always been a country girl at heart. I'm like my father. I love the land.''

''This is a far cry from what you're used to, Francesca.'' He felt driven to keep repeating it.

''Certainly,'' she agreed. ''Sheer *size* alone. It's a strange beauty. Primeval. One is constantly aware of the land's great antiquity but it's not alien to me. Don't you see that?''

''Francesca, you're classic English,'' he pointed out bluntly.

''And you just could be a classic stubborn Scot,'' she returned with a touch of fire.

He inclined his head in wry acknowledgment. ''Anyway I love your company. I love your calm, your patrician elegance and that little fiery streak that shows itself now and again.''

''But you're discouraging anything beyond close friendship?''

''Actually I think I'm behaving impeccably while we sort something out.''

"I'll remind you of that when you're married, secure and settled." She managed a smile. "But you haven't told me. What do you think of my idea of Myora for a homesite? It's spellbinding country."

"Don't you think I should consult my future bride?" he asked, a sardonic note in his voice.

"Not necessarily. Opal homestead has been lived in for generations. I'm part of everything. I'm descended from Cecilia Kinross who married her kinsman Ewan Kinross when she really loved Charles Cameron."

Grant groaned. "That story has been around for a long time."

"It must have been true. What do you think? There must have been some reason for Cecilia to turn her back on the man she loved? Then there was the famous opal-and-diamond necklace. Cecilia's Necklace. Both men Kinross and Cameron gave it to her."

"I love your accent." He digressed knowing where this was heading.

"I love yours, too." She barely paused. "The deep drawl until it gets very clipped. Anyway to continue the conversation maybe your ancestor allowed my ancestor to outmanoeuvre him. Maybe your ancestor tried to talk Cecilia out of staying in this country. It would have been hard indeed in the early days. He must have felt obliged to warn. He may have even urged her to go back to Scotland for her own good."

"Now why aren't I surprised you'd get around to saying that?" he asked a little caustically.

"I wonder what did happen?" She moved away a few feet, staring down at the spinifex-covered plains. The mirage was abroad, creating phantom hills, lakes and tall, sticklike nomads.

"My family believes there was a trick," Grant admitted after a pause. "Kinross managed to convince Cecilia his friend was promised to another woman, a woman far more suited to his way of life. The woman, in fact, Charles Cameron eventually married. But what does it matter now? Eventually the two families were reunited but the two men were never close again. It happens like that with betrayal. God knows a man like Stewart Kinross could have played that role." The accusation surged out, borne of many old resentments and griefs.

"But my grandfather wasn't like that," Francesca protested, recognising the hard kernel of truth in what Grant had said of her uncle Stewart. "Sir Andrew was greatly loved and respected."

It was perfectly true. "Sorry. I'm sorry, Francesca," Grant apologised. "Sir Andy was a fine man. Don't let's talk about ancient history anymore."

"It seems to me it has repercussions to this day," Francesca sighed. "Everyone gets stirred up when they talk about that old love affair."

"A love affair gone wrong." He spoke briskly. "Come back from that edge, there's a lot of loose shale."

"I'm no daredevil." She obeyed at once. "But it does have a compelling fascination."

"Tell me have you seen enough?" He was moved by her reactions, the great pleasure she had taken in their trip.

"For now. But you promised me a surprise."

"And I'm going to show it to you." He captured her hand again, so small in his, fingers so delicate. "We'll take another route down."

She would have missed the dome-shaped entrance to

the cave guarded as it was by a desert grevillea in full orange flower that appeared to grow out of sheer rock.

"We're here." Grant steadied her, though the ledge was fairly wide.

"Oh my goodness!" She felt a surge of excitement and anticipation. "Don't tell me, rock paintings?" She looked at him, willing him to say "yes!"

"This isn't a recorded site." He smiled at her enthusiasm. "There must be thousands all over the country. We like to keep ours a secret. It's not an important site but it's fascinating and it's been here since God knows when. The aborigines love to give colour and life to all of their shelters and caves. Inland hills, rocky outcrops, anywhere they can execute their art. A great many are in inaccessible places. It would be very easy to miss this. The family didn't know about this particular cave until fairly recently. Of course the local aborigines knew of its existence. Apparently they decided by my grandfather's time the Camerons had sufficient respect for traditional aboriginal culture to be told of its location."

"Why haven't I heard of this?" Francesca's expression was a mixture of awe and animation.

"You might have repeated the story all over." Grant drew back a large sage-green branch with its long, slender spines and masses of curly orange brushes exposing the wide, shallow entrance.

"Heavens you could have trusted me," Francesca said, peering in.

"I'm trusting you now," Grant's tone was dry. "I also want that ribbon you've got in your hair."

"Really?" She turned in surprise, standing stock-still as he reached out and pulled the ribbon from her thick upturned braid. Immediately the plait began to unravel and he smiled in beguilement, thinking she had the most wonderful hair he had ever seen. "Don't worry, Francesca, I'll give it back. For now I want to tie up this branch and let a bit of sun into the cave otherwise we won't have sufficient light."

"Keep the ribbon. A memento." It was a throwaway line but she found herself quivering at the look in his eyes, utterly brilliant, utterly desirous. She could not look away. She felt powerless to move. He tied the branch back, then he took her arm, moving her away from the neck of the cave. "Just stand out of harm's way for a moment while I check the interior. Some animal might have made the cave its home."

"As long as we're not talking bats." She gave a little shudder.

A moment more and he returned, so masculine, so vibrant, he stirred every deep feeling in her. "All clear. Actually I've forgotten how marvellous it is."

The instant they were inside the sandy-floored cave Francesca straightened up. Her eyes flashed around the ancient gallery that was covered in drawings. So many! The stone mass of the rear wall displayed highly stylised designs Francesca couldn't understand but found very attractive, executed in ochres, red, yellow, charcoal, black and white. On the ceiling, the highest point of the dome some eight feet, the designs were quite different. She understood immediately that they were male and delicate female figures in different aspects of making love watched over by what appeared to be totem beings or spirit figures. On the end walls were drawings of kangaroos, emus, mammals, reptiles, fish, birds and what seemed to be giant insects. Simple linear drawings but accurate and charming, the whole framed by impressions of human hands like a decoration.

"I can't possibly see this all in one day," she said her voice instinctively pitched low in deference to all these ancient symbols and ancestral beings. For all the drawings' simplicity this wasn't doodling in any shape or form. The rock paintings had a definite mystical power. The paintings relating directly to sex were even bringing the hot blood to her cheeks.

"So what do you suggest?" Grant's voice too was quiet with a faint shivery ring caused by the acoustics of the cave.

"Oh, God, I don't know! These are wonderful. Who else have you brought here?" She was aching for him to touch her, as sensations flashed through her body like so much sorcery. Weren't all those paintings supposed to mean love magic? Now there was a light wind blowing through the neck of the cave, adding its own hollow drumming, deep, soft notes reminiscent of the native didgeridoo, the wind's movements rippling the burnished sandy floor that she now saw had delicate, unusual patterns all over it. Spiders or little dragon lizards, she thought. Tracks recorded on the fine sand. Their tracks as well. Hers and Grant's. Her foot so much smaller.

"I expect a hundred girls," Grant said with a faint rasp.

"All of them in love with you?" She turned quickly, knowing without being told that she was the first woman outside family, except she was sure her cousin Ally, who had ever been brought here.

"I've never been in love in my life," he said, "except I'm afraid with *you*," he admitted almost roughly, a certain tension coming into his high-mettled face.

She had to clear her throat to speak. "And that's taboo?"

"That's how it is, Francesca."

One hand unconsciously went up to lie between her breasts. "You mean my title is a terrible constraint?"

"Your title is the smallest part of it," he said. "The *implications* of your title stronger, but overriding everything the near impossibility of transporting someone as delicate as you into a baked, red-glowing soil. It would take a miracle for you to survive."

His rejection was shattering. "So falling in love isn't enough?"

He groaned. "Think about it, Francesca. I beg you. Falling in love is agony. Allowing a woman to reach far into your mind and your body would be to give her all the power in the world."

She looked at him out of sparkling eyes. "So it hasn't happened yet?"

"I'm not going to let it get the better of me, Francesca," he warned.

Her heart was beating swiftly, to the point of pain. "So you think rules apply to people like me and you're not going to break them?"

He held up his hands, palms forward like a supplicant warding her off, yet his glance was magnetic, luring her on. "Don't look at me like that."

"Do you think I wanted this to happen, willed it to happen?"

"You couldn't have." He shook his head. "It happened all at once. Years ago when you were just a sweet little teenager."

"We were close then." Nostalgia was reflected in her voice.

"Aren't we closer now?" His own tone was regretful.

"But you want me to go?"

"As things are—" He broke off, intensely confused. On the one hand he was trying to do the right thing, on the other he was mad to take this woman and make her his. It had got to the point when he couldn't imagine life without her. It wasn't meant to happen like this. Not at all.

She gave a little cry that startled him. Then she was flinging herself backwards as a small brightly patterned dragon lizard lifted itself out of the deep sand, every spine on its head and back upraised, a fearsome little harmless thing, still with the ability to give an unsuspecting person a fright. It dashed at breakneck speed, across Francesca's foot and outside the cave.

"God, Fran, here." He caught her as she stumbled, sinking, sliding to the cave floor. "It's only a lizard. It can't hurt you." But he could. The fragrance of her body, that unique rose scent was everywhere. He thought constantly about making love to her. Now here she was in his arms, a featherweight, so utterly beautiful inside and out.

"I'm sorry. Sorry." She gave a little laugh that wasn't a laugh at all. More like a sob because it was all so sad, so ridiculous, so cruel.

Desperate for her now, Grant caught her up strongly, experiencing such passion he was drawn to cover her mouth fiercely, voluptuously, feeling it open...open, her breath as sweet as the desert breeze. The tip of her small tongue, barely lapping, danced around his, inciting him until he felt he couldn't stand it. He was hard with desire, bearing her slender body down onto the soft sand as if he had been waiting for this all his life.

"Francesca!" Everything about him was doing a slow, sizzling burn.

"Don't talk." Her white fingers came up to his lips. "Don't talk at all."

She allowed him to slip open the small pearly buttons of her pink shirt. He had never known such exquisite anticipation. He moved his hands over her small breasts, the rosy nipples already bunched tight to his touch. She was wearing some kind of white lacy thing like a little singlet beneath her shirt. Nothing else. Her breasts were perfect, small, taut, high, the skin like satin. He lowered his head and took first one nipple then the other into his mouth, hearing her soft, urgent moans, the most exciting and dangerous little sounds in the world.

Exactly what he feared was happening. He could get her pregnant. This beautiful creature. Yet his hand found the zip of her cotton jeans, drawing it down. His fingers moved in desperate caressing patterns over her velvet stomach to the apex of her body, a point he knew he shouldn't cross, but he did because he couldn't summon enough will to turn back.

Wonder. It was wonderful. And now he was quite, quite certain of what he had only suspected.

All the while he caressed her, his ministrations causing her to writhe, he studied her lovely face. Her eyes were closed, her head turned sideways, her hair a fiery bolt of silk across the sand.

Take her, he thought. Just take her. Give in to your greatest desire. You're both young and so much alive. So much in love. He couldn't deny it. She was too honest to try.

"Francesca, Francesca," he muttered in a mindless ecstasy, his mouth closing over hers again. She was extraordinary. A dream. He never imagined a woman could be so beautiful. He wanted to cover every inch of her with kisses. Kisses like little indelible marks that would stay on her body forever.

He smoothed his palm across her satin-smooth stomach. So flat. He imagined her having a child. His beautiful child. Boy or girl he wouldn't care. Such a child would surely have red-gold hair. A little innocent. Perfect in their eyes.

But seeing that child in his mind's eye brought him back to his senses at a powerful rush. Her slender white arms were thrown back, fingers digging into the sand. She couldn't stop that soft, little moan as his hunger had taken him deeper and deeper into exploring her body.

His hesitation was minimal but deeply painful as if he was gripped by cramps, but by sheer force of will he managed to move, retrieving the pink shirt he had thrown away, getting a handle on the deep clashing tumults inside of him.

"Francesca. Please. Come on." He coaxed her urgently but she kept her eyes shut, not responding. Somehow, unaided, he fixed the little singlet, got her shirt back on and buttoned, rezipped her jeans.

She didn't help him at all as if she had loved the way she was, half-naked and lost to him.

"You don't think this is easy for me, do you?" he pleaded, half-cursing his own principles. "This is harder than you'll ever know. But I have to stop, Francesca."

At last she showed some reaction by shaking her head. "Why?"

"How can you ask? How can I possibly know if the

time is right for you?'' he asked tautly. ''Are you on the pill or don't you care if you fall pregnant?''

She sat up immediately, clenching her small white teeth. ''I'm going to get a prescription right away.'' She was howling inside. Full of frustration.

''You have your virginity to bring to a man as a gift,'' he pointed out quietly.

''Damnation to that!''

He had to laugh, though the laugh went awry. ''I like it. It's pretty unusual these days.''

''It's the way I've chosen to live,'' she said, averting her head. ''I've never cared enough about anyone to let them get to the stage where they *know* me.''

He held her face between his hands and kissed her. ''So whatever happens some part of you will always be mine. Could I have made you pregnant today?''

A wild rose flush mounted her cheeks. She looked across the silent cave, her blue gaze falling on ancient couplings. ''I was too far gone to make notes.'' She tried a sad little joke. ''I suppose you expected better of me?''

Her expression was so poignant he reacted strongly. ''*I'm* the guilty one here, Francesca. I found the way to seduce you.''

''And you would have only you're blessed with an exceptionally strong will.''

''A year from now you might thank me.'' He stared into her face intently, committing every single feature to memory.

''I don't think so.'' She shook her head firmly, pushing her long hair back over her shoulders. ''I don't regret any of this, Grant Cameron. What I feel for you is in very short supply.''

CHAPTER FOUR

FOR days after Grant drove himself so hard, Brod, all his life honorary big brother, began to feel a niggling concern. There was no question Grant was splendidly fit, physically very strong, with nerves of steel, but it seemed to Brod he was putting himself under too much pressure without a safety valve. Cameron Airways now had sufficient pilots able and experienced enough to take over the big mustering jobs, but Grant was handling too much himself. It was a day in day out, dawn to dusk routine and not without its dangers especially for the helicopter pilot manoeuvring in difficult situations.

There was an undercurrent to all this. Brod was sure he knew what it was. *Francesca*. Grant had fallen very deeply in love with her but it was obvious to anyone who knew Grant well, he was taking it hard. It wasn't just a question of a young man used to a high level of self-sufficiency and freedom, fighting love's lasso. Grant seemed to be in genuine fear of hurting both of them by allowing their relationship to deepen.

Whatever happened the day he took Francesca off to Opal to see the cave—both had confided in him and of course as Rafe's best friend he had seen it—had been pivotal in their relationship. Of that Brod felt all but certain. There was a kind of shining innocence about Francesca, a definable purity that remained. But something fairly traumatic had happened.

Midafternoon when the men were relaxing over billy

tea and fresh damper, hot from the coals, Brod drew Grant aside.

"Why don't we go down there?" He indicated a fallen log like a giant bonsai on the sandy shore of the creek, with its spreading green signifying the return of the good seasons.

Grant followed him gratefully. Rarely tired, he found himself curiously drained. "All right with you if Jock McFadden finishes tomorrow?" he asked, as soon as they were settled, a fragrant mug of tea in hand, a couple of the cattle dogs, Bluey and Rusty, curled at their feet.

"No problem at all." Brod pushed his akubra back on his head, turning to look at his friend. "Is everything okay?"

Grant smiled wryly. "Now why do you sound like Rafe?"

"Do I?" Brod's grin displayed his beautiful white teeth. "Well, Rafe's away."

"So you're his deputy. Anyway I meant to tell you—" Grant swallowed a mouthful "—had a phone call from them last night. Early hours of the morning actually."

"Both well?" Brod watched him expectantly.

"On top of the world. They're on the West Coast now. Los Angeles. And guess who they met up with in the street?" His hazel eyes sparkled with amusement and pleasure.

"Any clues?"

"One." Grant nodded. "When we were kids he was considered an even bigger rebel than me."

Brod laughed. "In that case it would have to be your cousin, Rory."

"Got it in one." Grant took another deep gulp, realising he was parched. "Rory Cameron."

"Would have been at Rafe's wedding only he was taking a little hike up Everest wasn't he?" Brod asked.

Grant nodded. "What words can you use to describe that? He's fearless, Rory. I'd love to do it myself. He went up with a New Zealand party. Rory's a real adventurer. There's nowhere he hasn't been from the Himalayas to the Amazonian jungle. His dad thinks he'll never settle down."

Sammy Lee, part aboriginal part Chinese camp cook arrived with slices of damper and jam, which both took.

"It's a good thing then Rory has an elder brother to take over the running of Rivoli," Brod remarked dryly after Sammy had gone. Rivoli was one of the Northern Territory's biggest cattle stations owned and run by Grant's uncle, stepbrother to his late father.

"Josh is a great guy," Grant agreed, "but he hasn't got Rory's enormous *zest*. There's a guy who's brimming over with life. Anyway would you believe it, he's coming home?"

"Lord, he's been away years. He's going to find it tame, settling in the one place, if that's what he intends to do."

"Don't spread it around but I aim to talk him into joining me," Grant told Brod confidentially. "I got to thinking about it last night after the call. Rory's a great pilot. Every last Cameron has a head for business. I could use a man like Rory."

Brod shook his head doubtfully. "No way he'd come into anything without being a full partner."

"You're not wrong! But no harm in discussing it. Rory's my cousin, a Cameron. I know for a fact he got all old Digby Cameron's money. That makes him a rich man. Anyway we'll see. Needless to say Rafe and Ally send you and Rebecca their love. I spoke to Rafe too about Francesca's idea of doing those outback location shots on Opal.''

Brod finished off his mug of tea and signalled for another. ''What did he say?''

''He doesn't mind. In fact he supports it if I negotiate a good deal and the money goes to the Bush Rescue trust.''

Brod nodded his approval. ''Rafe's doing a wonderful job with that. Now that Dad's gone Kimbara will enter the scheme. Rafe and I discussed it. Even if we save one kid and put them on the right path it's worth it.''

''Well it's working.'' Grant paused to thank Sammy who was back pouring fresh tea.

''So what are you going to do tomorrow?'' Brod returned to his main concern. ''Take some time off. It seems to me you've hit a cracking pace.''

''I won't have Francesca over to visit if that's what you mean.'' Grant shot him a sidelong glance.

''What's the problem?'' Brod was equally direct. ''Aren't you two in love?''

''God, love! What *is* love?'' Grant muttered in a kind of anguish.

''I'd say what *you feel*,'' Brod responded. ''You're not just in love with my cousin. You love her. You're tormenting yourself with what you consider is appropriate.''

''It shows?'' asked Grant, not smiling.

''Hell, Grant, I've known you all your life. I know how a man feels, when he's faced with a big emotional decision. I know you're a man of integrity. I know I can trust you with Francesca. I know you would never consciously hurt her."

Grant gestured wearily. "I'm wrong for her, Brod."

"Why?" Brod damned nearly shouted. "The consensus of opinion is you're an exceptional young man. You have real standing in the outback community. That's not all that easy to earn."

"Down here. Down here, I'm worried." Grant struck his chest. "If she were any other girl! I want her as much as it's possible to want a woman, but she's like some enchanting creature from another planet. Even her colouring scares me."

Brod shook his head, halfway between disbelief and understanding. "Grant, get a balance here. Your own father had red hair. Your mother was very blonde. Look at you and Rafe. Don't all the girls call you the golden boys?"

Grant studied the glint of hair on his forearms. "We've had generations to acclimatise. We've grown hardy. We're *natives*. Francesca is like some rare exotic no one in their right mind would plant here. She can't survive. The big heat is ahead. You know as well as I do, Brod, the mercury can hit forty-eight degrees!"

Brod looked up at the cloudless, peacock-blue sky. "We don't expect our womenfolk to go out in the midday sun, whatever Noel Coward had to say. Times have changed greatly. We have so much now, so many aids we've never had before. It's been a technological revolution."

"Maybe. But the fact remains no one is going to be able to change the desert environment."

"Between the two of us," Brod said wryly, "I don't want to change it. I love my home like no other place on earth."

Grant responded with a sudden spurt of passion. "Don't get me wrong. I love it, too. We've learned to love it. We thrive on it. But Francesca is a very special person. I'm determined to protect her."

"Hell, Grant, if you keep this up you'll drive her away," Brod warned. "You'll lose her. Are you prepared to risk that?"

Grant's handsome, determined features tautened. "I'd rather lose her now than lose her later on. That would kill me. What if we were married and she decided one day she longed for everything she had lost? Everything she had ever known and understood? She's no *ordinary* girl."

"An ordinary girl wouldn't suit you, Grant. Have you thought of that?" Brod suggested dryly.

Grant shook his head. "I don't know any other girl of her particular background. Surely it couldn't be more different from ours?"

"So you don't think she's adult enough to make up her own mind?" Irony crackled in Brod's tone.

"You realise any son she may have could be her father's heir?"

Brod gave a faint smile. "So what? As far as I know, Francesca's father is having the devil of a job trying to keep Ormond intact. The upkeep must be crippling. Especially without Fee's money. Fee was the heiress. For that matter, still is."

"You don't see anything tremendously threatening about our relationship?" Grant asked, realising this conversation was going some way to easing his mind.

Brod took his time replying. Then he spoke very seriously, from the depths of his soul. "I think when you find someone you truly love you never let them go."

* * *

In amongst all his thinking, and he had lots on his mind—an upcoming meeting with Drew Forsythe of Trans Continental Resources for one—he kept drawing mental plans of his dream homestead. Of course he'd need an architect to walk the site, gauge just the right spot for the house to go. There were vast, sweeping views from everywhere nevertheless siting the homestead properly would present a challenge. Without fully realising it his mind was extraordinarily visual so his intermittent daydreams really came alive. He wanted the house set on low pylons like Opal but there the similarity ended, except for the mandatory wide verandahs to shelter the core of the house from the heat and sun at the same time as providing deep shade and cooling breezes.

He wanted his homestead radically different. He wanted a completely contemporary structure using a mix of materials: stone, glass—lots of glass, floor to ceiling—steel to support the long spans of verandah, the polished timbers he loved, local stone with all its wonderful ochres, especially for the fireplaces. The really hard thing would be to come up with a design worthy of the great wilderness bounded as it was by the great rolling parallel waves of the desert, unobstructed views over the plains to the horizon with the legendary Myora for a background. How many people had an awe-inspiring prehistoric monolithic rock in their backyard. A backyard that ran on forever.

He had visited the island of Bali many times, loved it, and found Balinese influences creeping into his thinking, though the lush jungle settings could scarcely be more different from Opal. But the harmonious feeling of timbers, open spaces, high tentlike ceilings, open pavilions was the same. Like Bali, too, nights in the

Dry could be surprisingly cold as the desert sands lost their heat. He would need those couple of huge, inviting fireplaces. In every room he saw Francesca, however much he tried to picture some other woman.

Lord knows he knew enough attractive girls. They swarmed to the polo meets. There was a time he felt quite happy with Jennie Irvine. Her father, Tom Irvine, the well-known pastoralist, had been a good friend to his own father. Jennie was good-looking, well educated, easygoing, fun to be with. He knew he could get Jennie to marry him. He knew her parents would be really happy about it but someone called Francesca de Lyle had put paid to that. By Brod's wedding he had really known Francesca had stolen his heart.

She was like some irresistible fragrance. All those silly ads he had seen about perfume and the way they enticed a man weren't so silly after all. Francesca was a rose, to him the most beautiful, the most fragrant of all flowers.

Even his dreams were set at this homestead that had yet to be built. Vividly he saw Francesca at the breakfast table, having a cup of coffee with him. Francesca in the glowing panelled dining room playing hostess to family and friends. Francesca in the study reading over his shoulder as he drafted an important letter, welcoming her input because he valued her opinion and good business sense. Most of all he saw her in the bedroom, lying on top of their huge bed, a modern four-poster hung with curtains of white netting against any little insects that might fly through all the open doorways. For some reason he never saw his Francesca naked. She was always wearing the prettiest, beribboned, most feminine nightgown, a swirl of peach silk, he would lovingly peel off.

We'd like to send you **2 FREE** novels and a surprise gift to introduce you to Harlequin Romance®. Accept our special offer today and

Indulge in a Harlequin Moment!

HOW TO QUALIFY:

1. With a coin, carefully scratch off the silver area on the card at right to see what we have for you—**2 FREE BOOKS** and a **FREE GIFT—ALL YOURS! ALL FREE!**

2. Send back the card and you'll receive two brand-new Harlequin Romance® novels. These books have a cover price of $3.50 each in the U.S. and $3.99 each in Canada, but they are yours to keep absolutely free!

3. There's no catch. You're under no obligation to buy anything. We charge nothing—ZERO—for your first shipment and you don't have to make any minimum number of purchases—not even one!

4. The fact is, thousands of readers enjoy receiving books by mail from the Harlequin Reader Service®. They enjoy the convenience of home delivery... they like getting the best new novels at discount prices, BEFORE they're available in stores...and they love their *Heart to Heart* subscriber newsletter featuring author news, horoscopes, recipes, book reviews and much more!

5. We hope that after receiving your free books you'll want to remain a subscriber. But the choice is yours—to continue or cancel, any time at all. So why not take us up on our invitation with no risk of any kind. You'll be glad you did!

SPECIAL FREE GIFT!

We can't tell you what it is...but we're sure you'll like it! A FREE gift just for giving the **Harlequin Reader Service**® a try!

Visit us online at
www.eHarlequin.com

The **2 FREE BOOKS** we
send you will be selected from
HARLEQUIN ROMANCE®,
the series that brings you love
stories that capture the essence
of traditional romance.

Books received may vary.

Scratch off the
silver area to see
what the Harlequin
Reader Service
has for you.

HARLEQUIN®
Makes any time special™

I have scratched off the silver area above.
Please send me the **2 FREE** books and
gift for which I qualify. I understand I am
under no obligation to purchase any
books, as explained on the back and
on the opposite page.

YES!

NAME   (PLEASE PRINT CLEARLY)

ADDRESS

APT.#   CITY

STATE/PROV.   ZIP/POSTAL CODE

386 HDL C4HH   **186 HDL C4G7**
                                    (H-R-OS-09/00)

Offer limited to one per household and not valid to current
Harlequin Romance® subscribers. All orders subject to approval.

THE HARLEQUIN READER SERVICE®—Here's how it works:

Accepting your 2 free books and gift places you under no obligation to buy anything. You may keep the books and gift and return the shipping statement marked "cancel." If you do not cancel, about a month later we'll send you 6 additional novels and bill you just $2.90 each in the U.S., or $3.34 each in Canada, plus 25¢ shipping & handling per book and applicable taxes if any.* That's the complete price and — compared to cover prices of $3.50 each in the U.S. and $3.99 each in Canada — it's quite a bargain! You may cancel at any time, but if you choose to continue, every month we'll send you 6 more books, which you may either purchase at the discount price or return to us and cancel your subscription.

*Terms and prices subject to change without notice. Sales tax applicable in N.Y. Canadian residents will be charged applicable provincial taxes and GST.

What a fool! At this point he always woke himself up. Falling in love with Francesca was bliss and despair. Her destiny like his was already written. Dreams had little to do with real life. That was the unpalatable fact. The reality of the situation was, he was acting out a fantasy and heading for disaster. Love had to be matched by other factors that would make a marriage survive.

Francesca was a beautiful, bright superior creature, carefully guarded by her father and clearly destined for a privileged life similar to the one she had led. How could he hold such a woman in isolation? The polar caps could melt before he tired of her but what if she found his way of life far too lonely and distant from all she had known? Despite his conversation with Brod he still was deeply affected by practical constraints as a man who was making a decision that would affect his whole life had to be.

He didn't need to be a mind-reader, either, to guess Francesca's father would be utterly and completely against such a marriage and why not? It would take his only beloved child away from him. Halfway across the world. As far away as she could go. Shatter his plans. Fee had all but admitted that. So problems continued to beset his euphoria. Women seemed conditioned by nature to take great leaps into the unknown. For a man it was different. A man's duty was to keep his feet on the ground.

The film people arrived at the weekend, staying over at Kimbara, which with its many guest rooms at the ready was far better suited to accommodating guests than Opal; Ngaire Bell, the New Zealand born director, who was making quite a name for herself internationally, accompanied by long-time associate and script writer, Glenn Richards. Grant was kept busy all day Saturday working out schedules for incoming jobs, double-checking maintenance, arranging freight pick-ups, a workload that kept him on Opal but sunset found him landing on Kimbara preparatory to meeting Brod and Rebecca's guests at dinner.

Francesca was there to greet him, dressed in jeans and a yellow T-shirt, her hair burning like flame in the incandescent light.

"Hi, this is nice!" He bent to kiss her cheek, thinking "nice" was a ridiculous word. He was just plain thrilled to see her. She made his heart run hot.

"It's lovely to see you, too," she responded. "It's been a very long week."

"Lots to do." He spoke casually, throwing his hold-all in the back seat of the Jeep, not mentioning he had found the time away from her a near eternity. "So what are the guests like?" he asked as they got under way, Francesca at the wheel, small hands but capable and confident.

"I know you're going to like them." Francesca turned her head half-laughing now with pleasure. "Ngaire is a very interesting woman. She and Fee are getting along famously. Glenn is good company, too. Rebecca and he have a lot in common."

"And what about you?"

"I'm happy. I'm really happy," she said, eyes alight. "We're all getting along well but of course the others have special interests in common."

"How old, I wonder?" He spoke lightly, companionably when all he wanted to do was wrap her in his arms.

"Ngaire, late thirties, early forties. Naturally I didn't ask. Glenn would be around thirty-five."

"Married?" He wanted this guy married. He refused to confront why.

"Neither of them are married," Francesca said. "They're great friends and colleagues but I wouldn't think they were romantically involved. Of course I could be wrong. You didn't want to kiss me?"

Because if I did I wouldn't stop. "Kissed your cheek, didn't I?" he said.

"So you did. It was nice, too. How glorious the sunsets are out here," she said, examining the sky.

"Like your hair." He successfully resisted touching it. "If you want to see a sight, cut off the track now and head north-west for about a mile. The black swans should be heading in for their roosting sites at dusk."

"So where are we going?" Where the heck *is* north-east, she thought. She'd have to ask him to show her.

"Here, let me."

They stopped to swop positions, Grant driving, Francesca in the passenger seat of the open Jeep. "Kingurra. You must know it," Grant said a few moments later, the Jeep exploding into action.

"Lake Kingurra?" She cast a glance at his golden profile. Like Rafe he had a cleft chin, the cleft not so deep but vertical.

"The very one," he teased. "Kingurra means black swan. Didn't you know that?"

She shook her head. "The straight answer is no. There's so much *to* know. It would take a lifetime. Even learning all the aboriginal names."

"They're the ones I like best. Our aboriginal brothers have been custodians of this country for over sixty thousand years. Kingurra is a very old lake, a real oasis of wildlife.''

"Of course I've seen it," Francesca said. "It's astonishingly beautiful especially with the area all around it so arid.''

"Listen *now*." Grant leant towards her, his expression full of the pleasure of sharing.

They heard the birds before they saw them, the sound carried on the sweet evening breeze. The dark shadows became hundreds of black swans skeining across the darkening mauve sky still banded with the brilliant rose, gold and scarlet of the desert sunset.

"What a sight!" Francesca lifted her head, staring, fascinated by the pure white underwings of the ebony birds, the little band of turquoise, the red beaks. The *S* bends of their beautiful necks were fully outstretched, straight as arrows.

"We've got time to take a walk down to the water," Grant said, picking up speed and heading away from the mulga scrub to the lake.

A little bit of excitement went a long way. "It might sound extraordinary but I'm rarely away from the homestead at this hour," Francesca explained, her cheeks pink. "If I go riding or driving around the property Brod likes me home before dusk."

Grant shot her a shimmering glance. "So would I if you were on your own. Night falls as dramatically as a black curtain. But this is worth seeing and I'm with you."

He held her hand all the while they descended the sandy track crisscrossed with the prints of kangaroos and smaller creatures. Quietly, quietly, they kept to the cover of the trees so as not disturb the birds.

There were hundreds of them! Squadrons splashing

down on the silver lake, while others circled just like aircraft waiting for landing. Two hundred or more stately pelicans had congregated at the far end of the lake, keeping their distance from the common ducks, the cormorants, egrets, banded stilts and so many species Francesca couldn't possibly identify them. As the swans landed, they sealed off their white underwings, bending their long necks into the beautiful curves of legends. They remained, united by their great pleasure in the scene, familiar to Grant all his life, though he never tired of it, a rare enchantment for Francesca.

The outback *was* birds. She adored watching the great flights of budgerigar, the parrots and galahs, the flocks of white corellas that literally covered the trees, but she had never seen so many water birds congregated in the one place. It was like some wonderful harbour, the waters that swirled with birds gradually blanketed in feathers.

"This is wonderful!" she whispered.

"I agree." His head was bent over hers, his breath warm against her ear.

"Thank you for bringing me here."

"I'm amazed you've missed it on your visits."

Not so many, she thought with regret. She'd first come to Kimbara at the age of ten. Her father didn't want her to come. He told her Australia was a far country. *Strange.* He told her her mother's people lived in the desert. Were barely civilised. Yet her mother was the most beautiful most glamorous creature she had ever seen.

When she arrived on Kimbara it was like coming home. She wasn't drawn to it. It didn't take time. She loved it at once. It was almost like her spirit had been unleashed. She was a very lonely little girl. Although her father tried to do everything he could, when she wasn't away at boarding school, she was left to her own devices a great deal.

"Coming to Australia was the greatest adventure of my life," she murmured aloud. "Still is for that matter."

"What about the heat, little Titian head?" he gently mocked.

"The heat could never exhaust my excitement. Not now. Not then. It's *dry* heat, isn't it? Not steamy, enervating heat."

It was true she always looked as cool as a lily. "Well, I'm glad you enjoyed your visit," he said lightly, "but we'd better go." *Before I give in to the desire to kiss you until you're panting and incoherent.*

They crouched low beneath some overhanging branches, finding their way back up the slope, Francesca forging ahead with a buoyant step. They almost arrived at the top when suddenly Grant grasped her firmly from behind, locking an arm around her waist, stopping her short.

"What is it?" Now he lifted her clean off the ground, holding her with one arm as though she were still a ten-year-old.

He didn't answer for a moment, then he set her down again with a nonchalant, "Nothing!"

She had to lean back against him momentarily unsteady. "You gave me such a fright."

"Better that than let you tread on a snake," he drawled. "There it goes. Off by the rocks."

"Lord!" Her expression sharpened with dread, as she strained back against him.

"Harmless, that one," Grant told her. "It was only

trying to get across the track. Snakes flee man in general. It doesn't do to step on one all the same.''

She gave a little shudder, turning within the circle of his arm, banging him on his chest in an instinctive response to fright. "I suppose you think I'm silly?"

He slipped his hand around her wrist and felt the delicate bones. "No, I think you're enormously brave." He gazed down into her eyes, eyes that seemed to see further into him than anyone else. "I'm sorry I scared you."

"I'm not scared," she breathed. And now she wasn't. "I'm here with you."

Inside he fought a violent struggle but he lost it. He lowered his head blindly, ravenously, taking her sweet gorgeous mouth, devouring it deeply, hungrily, luscious as a peach.

My God, I love her! he thought, abandoning himself to the ecstasy. Why the hell didn't he just hang on to that instead of making a terror out of all their difference.

"At least we've got one thing in common," he muttered, when he found the strength to lift his head.

"Lots!" She could only manage one word, her heart hammering, her breath drowned in her throat.

After a minute she was able to open her eyes. "We've got lots of things in common," she protested with soft vehemence. "Don't push me away, Grant," she warned, and he had never seen her more serious. "I've been pushed away all my life."

The next moment she turned, straightened the T-shirt his caressing hands had somehow pulled askew, and ran from him leaving him utterly sobered, staring after her.

Pushed away all her life! How was that possible?

From all accounts her father adored her. He had big plans for her. Fee was Fee. Not the most maternal of women but it couldn't be plainer she loved her beautiful daughter. It struck him like an actual blow Francesca could ever feel rejected. Francesca was a miracle. She touched his mind, his body, his heart with her exquisite grace.

They all came together in the very grand drawing room for a predinner drink, Brod introducing Grant to his guests.

"My God!" Ngaire Bell thought as they shook hands. These cattle kings are something else! A distinct breed. To begin with they had such an aura of masculinity they really made a woman *feel* like a woman. Moreover they made direct eye contact with far-seeing, delightfully sun-crinkled eyes. Broderick Kinross was an extraordinarily handsome man. She truly hadn't expected anyone else to match him yet here was this fabulous-looking man with the rarest of colourings.

On their looks alone she could make stars of them, she thought wryly, only it couldn't have been more obvious they exactly matched their setting. They were outback men yet they lived in great style.

Kimbara homestead was splendid, meticulously maintained, but too grandly furnished for the homestead of her new movie. It had been suggested to her by Fee Kinross's beautiful daughter, Francesca, the homestead at Opal Downs would fit readily the description of the sprawling, elegant old homestead of the novel, its Victorian furnishings still largely in place, the atmosphere retained. She was dying to see it. Couldn't wait. This wasn't the first historic mansion she had been invited to but this was the furthest into the continent's Wild Heart. It fired her already fertile imagination.

Glenn Richards, drink in hand, was thinking much the same thing as his friend and colleague. These Kinross-Camerons were an extraordinarily good-looking bunch. He had to put it down to the desert air. Even Fiona Kinross, who had to be in her sixties, looked marvellous. In the flattering light no more than forty-five. Of course she could have had cosmetic surgery, but he didn't think so. Nevertheless her skin was unlined, her jawline firm, her figure in a neat jade knee-length dress, excellent. She cut a glamorous figure as did they all, including Fiona's brand-new fiancé, David Westbury, tall, distinguished, pewter haired, very upper class English. As far as Glenn could make out, Westbury was a relative of sorts, and he was a touch overawed, trying to click in all his various impressions.

But the one who really took his eye and had from the very first moment, was the Lady Francesca. As far as he was concerned she was quite lovely. He adored her soft, dreamy looks, the uncontrived sensuality that made a man drool. And that colouring. He couldn't think of a more heavenly combination than red-gold hair and sky-blue eyes. Not a freckle in sight. Not even a gold dusting across her nose.

It struck him she would be perfect in the movie as the hero's tragic first wife. What made it even better was she had the authentic English accent. Maybe a bit too cut glass but that could be modified slightly. It was only a small part. They had more or less settled on Paige Macauly but he was certain if the girl could act at all she would be perfect in the role. And why wouldn't she be able to act with Fiona Kinross for a mother, let alone her cousin, Ally, who proved she didn't have what it took to make the big time by going off and getting married. What a waste!

Still, their leading lady Caro Halliday, wife number two in the film, who didn't feature in the early outback scenes, was beautiful, talented and almost as charismatic. As they went into dinner, Glenn began to turn over ideas in his mind. He'd put a lot of hard work into the screenplay. A lot of his own money went into the backing. It was crucial the film do well not only as an "art" film but as entertainment for the masses. The English rose, Francesca was enormously appealing, beautiful but nonthreatening. She had as much appeal as her far more exotic mother.

Grant, as sensitive to Francesca as it was possible to be, honed in immediately on Richards's interest in her. It was all managed with charm and a certain suavity but Richards couldn't keep his eyes off her. Not that Grant could blame him no matter how it made him inwardly bristle. Francesca looked ethereal in a delicate lace dress, the soft apricot of his dreams. She had left her hair out, too, in the way he loved it, long and flowing.

It wasn't the first time he had seen Francesca capture a whole lot of male attention but it was the first time another man had provoked his male aggression. Francesca was *his*. Immediately, as he thought it, he was forced to confront his own contradictions. He had no rights where Francesca was concerned. She was a free agent. As was he and apparently Glenn Richards. But no question about it, Richards's eyes on Francesca had set him off. Richards wasn't even being terribly discreet, his dark eyes savouring Francesca's appearance and the quality of her conversation. Which seemed reasonable enough given Francesca showed her intelligence and breeding, but he was starting to fill Grant with an odd hostility he tried to fight down.

Richards was an attractive man—dark curly hair, deep brown eyes, quirky eyebrows, an easy, friendly smile, midheight, well dressed, well-travelled, clever and articulate. Nothing there to dislike except he was taking far too much interest in Francesca. Grant felt a need to sort out his emotions before they got out of hand. He knew he had an aggressive streak. He knew he had to keep it under control.

They were seated in the formal dining room with its fine paintings and furnishings. Ngaire started out by commenting on the exquisite floral arrangement at the centre of the table, and reached to stroke a petal. Rebecca smiled her pleasure. "Francesca must take the credit. We spent some time over the arrangements, experimenting with containers and the various shapes for the flowers."

"Yes, I noticed," Ngaire said as indeed she had. "The arrangement in the main hall is quite dramatic."

"I'm afraid we robbed the Golden Shower tree." Francesca smiled. "A few palms, gold ribbon. A wonderful big Chinese vase. We had a lot of fun."

"Ikebana isn't it?" Ngaire asked, thinking how beautiful and stylish all the arrangements through the house were.

"I actually took a course with a master teacher a few years back," Rebecca said. "I must say Fran is an apt pupil. The centrepiece is inspirational."

"I agree." Brod looked like he thought his wife and cousin could do anything they turned their hand to.

"A mangrove root, dracena and a couple of sprays of white butterfly orchids, plus some red wire for a bit of dash," Francesca said, identifying the materials she

had used. "It means something, too. I quote from I
don't know where. Probably anonymous. 'Happiness is
like a butterfly. The more you chase it the more it will
elude you, but if you turn your attention to other things,
it will come and softly sit on your shoulder.'"
Somehow it seemed appropriate. Her gaze met Grant's
enigmatically across the table. "Of course, too, it's a
symbol of welcome."

"Yes, indeed. Welcome to Kimbara, Ngaire and
Glenn." Brod raised his wineglass and the others fol-
lowed suit. "Tomorrow you'll see Opal, my sister
Ally's new home. It has its own wonderful appeal as
you're due to find out. In our childhood Opal was
Ally's and my second home."

"In fact we were all so close we were family."
Grant gave a truly illuminating smile. "Now we are
family. The Camerons and the Kinrosses united at
last."

"There's such a fascination about your stories,"
Ngaire said. "Two great pioneering dynasties. I can't
wait to read your biography, Fee."

"Don't worry, darling," Fee said in her deep sexy
voice. "You and Glenn are invited to our preview
party. It was a brainwave on Fran's part thinking of
Opal for the colonial outback scenes. I was re-reading
The Immigrant last night. The station is close to perfect
for Bruce Templeton's book."

Grant nodded. "I've read the novel as well and thoroughly enjoyed it. With a few minor changes the homestead will serve you well. You're lucky Ally hadn't got
started on all her refurbishing. My mother intended to
make them but never got the chance."

"I'm so sorry, Grant," Ngaire murmured, aware his

parents had been tragically killed in an air crash. "I can't wait to visit tomorrow," she added gently.

The meal Rebecca and Francesca had worked on for a couple of days before the guests arrived, progressed splendidly with help in the kitchen: crab cream for starters, with crisp fried vermicelli followed by tournedos of Kimbarra beef with roast parsnips and potatoes, fresh green beans and two sauces, madeira and béarnaise. The conversation flowed over a wide range of subjects: the movie, Fee's role in it, Fee's and David's impending nuptials, Grant's vision for Cameron Airways, outback life, Rafe and Ally's overseas honeymoon, domestic politics, world politics, a smattering of gossip, books that had not made an easy transition into movies.

Everyone took part, full of animated interest as the wineglasses quickly emptied. Francesca, as usual, limited herself to two. She noticed Rebecca did the same, but Fee sipped her wine quickly, glass after glass, showing no effects except her beautiful, slender hands moved even more expressively and her green eyes glittered with great good humour. This was an area where Fee shone, and David looked on, his heart swelling with pride. After the last few sad years Fee was a positive joy to him.

There was a choice for dessert—chocolate sorbet and orange ice-cream or an Old English apple pie, richly flavoured with dark brown sugar, nutmeg, cinnamon, orange and lemon zest, raisins and sultanas, served with double cream. This was David's contribution to the meal from a family recipe he had enjoyed from childhood. He knew all the ingredients, even if he didn't know exact quantities. He even stood beside

Francesca in the kitchen while she made it saying he always liked his with cheddar cheese.

Mellowed by such a wonderful meal, Glenn took the opportunity to say what he'd been thinking for the past two hours.

"It was a wonderful coup securing you for a pivotal role, Fiona—" he deferred to her "—you'll bring great presence and credibility to the role, but I can't help thinking your beautiful daughter, Francesca, would make a marvellous Lucinda."

"Hey, that's amazing!" Ngaire burst out, but Fee stared at Glenn in astonishment, her spoon frozen in midair.

"Fran doesn't *act,* Glenn," she said as though it were completely out of character. "She's had no training whatsoever. Ally is the only other actress in the family."

"And she's marvellous, too," Glenn said, still getting over his disappointment Ally Kinross had rejected the lead.

But Ngaire waved a hand. "Training is important, of course, Fee, but I know for a fact some people are naturals. The fourteen-year-old I had in my last movie was sensational. Straight from school though she was learning drama and art of speech."

"But Fran has no interest in acting, have you, darling?" Fee looked down the table, clearly unable to picture her daughter as an actress. "She's much happier with her drawing and her music. She's very good at both. Francesca is the product of a very good school."

Grant turned his iridescent eyes on Francesca. "I didn't know that," he said, sounding like he wished he had.

"Now that we've settled down I'll get a good piano sent out here," Brod said briskly.

"Make it a Steinway." Francesca smiled at him.

"Then a Steinway it is." Brod was quite serious. "I know you *draw* extremely well."

"What about acting?" Glenn persisted, fingering his wineglass. The sauterne was wonderful. "Surely they put on plays at your very good school?"

Francesca nodded her head. "Of course they did. Mamma's going to be amazed but I was very much in demand. A lot of Shakespeare. I was a fabulous Juliet," she joked, "to my friend, Dinah Phillip's Romeo. Pity you didn't see us."

"*Why* didn't I see you?" Fee demanded.

"Ah, Mamma," Francesca murmured, rolling her eyes.

"You mean I wasn't around?" Fee gazed off into the middle distance remembering how it was.

"You were lighting up the London stage," Francesca reminded her.

"Now I think about it you *could* play Lucinda." Grant's voice had gathered conviction.

"I agree," Ngaire murmured.

"You really think Francesca could handle it?" Fee stared at Ngaire as though she had gone mad.

"I'd love to," Francesca said

"You could handle it, I know you could." Grant looked across the table at Francesca thinking Fee was the last straw. "It would be good for you. A bit of fun, widen your horizons."

"Surely, darling, you wouldn't entertain the idea of acting as a career?" Grant might as well have suggested prostitution.

"No, Mamma, I wouldn't." Francesca shook her

head, her manner gentle but firm. "It's more as Grant says. A bit part. A bit of fun."

"A challenge." Grant smiled, always one for a challenge, good, too, at encouraging others. "You're full of surprises, Francesca. Full of refinements. I'd *love* to hear you play the piano." No wonder he always heard music flow around her.

"So you shall," Brod promised. "There was a grand piano here in my mother's day. She played beautifully, but my father got rid of it. He wouldn't let Ally learn, either," he added a trifle bleakly, "though she wanted to."

"I expect it was too painful," Ngaire murmured, not knowing the full story.

"But surely you have that NADA graduate, what's her name, Paige something?" Fee carried on with her objections.

"Paige Macauly," Glenn supplied. "Yes, Paige was well in the running but we've made no final decision, have we, Ngaire."

"I thought we had, dear," Ngaire said wryly. "But I quite share your vision of Francesca as Lucinda. One can see her in the part."

"I get killed off early," Francesca said. "I could do a good job of pining away. Isn't that what I'm supposed to do. Pine away in a strange new country?"

Glenn smiled. "Of course your character was never very strong. Physically you suggest fragility, sensitivity."

Francesca didn't see herself as quite the marshmallow. "Ballerinas are very fragile looking," she pointed out, "but they're very strong. I'll have you know I play an excellent game of tennis. There was a time I was good at archery. I'm a very good rider, aren't I, Brod?"

She appealed to her cousin who was always on her side.

"A lovely seat on a horse. Sweet hands," Brod agreed. "A woman's looks can belie her strengths."

"So what about reading for the part?" Glenn pressed on as keen to get to know Francesca better as to have her in a role that would keep her in daily contact.

"I must say, Glenn, I think you're going too fast," Fee protested. "Francesca's father wouldn't be at all happy about another actress in the family. One was more than enough."

"It's only a bit part, Mamma," Francesca said reassuringly.

"Yes, but you might get the bug."

It was hard to say what was really bothering Fee, David thought. Fear Francesca could cause herself some embarrassment? He couldn't see *how*. Or fear of de Lyle's wrath. As far as he was concerned his cousin was of an age she could do as she pleased. Probably very well.

It was difficult for Grant to get Francesca alone until well after eleven when Brod excused himself from the conversation saying he had a dawn start. Station work went on seven days a week and though the staff had a roster Brod did not. Rebecca, too, excused herself with a charming smile leaving Fee to carry on with the conversation, which reverted to an in-depth discussion of the film, characterisation and so forth.

It was time to grab Francesca and run, Grant thought, aware of Richards's acute disappointment when she left the charmed circle, though Fee talked on, her chain of thought unbroken.

"I think you've won yourself a heart," Grant commented dryly as they walked down the front steps to take a short stroll.

Francesca ignored that, picking up on what really concerned her. "Mamma didn't sound too pleased with Glenn's suggestion," she said, her own pleasure eroded by her mother's reaction.

"I think you're going to be brilliant," Grant said, mutually upset by Fee. "You're vibrantly artistic. I don't like to say it but Fee seems to be devoid of sensitivity sometimes."

"She isn't always tactful," Francesca was forced to agree. "Maybe she thinks I'm going to make a goose of myself. Or worse a goose of her."

He drew her to him, one arm lightly around her waist. "You want to do it, don't you?"

Francesca felt a lot easier in his company. "Yes, but not if Mamma would rather I didn't."

"You're a big girl now, Francesca," he pointed out, his voice oddly tender.

"I've never been much good at upsetting people."

"Don't feel guilty about Fee," he warned.

"So what do you think I should do?" she spoke softly, but sounding pained.

"I've told you. Go for it. You'll enjoy it." His arm tightened in a hug.

"And what if I get bitten by the bug as Mamma seems to think?" She knew she wouldn't. Her priorities had been long since fixed.

"If you get hooked, you get hooked," Grant answered lightly, thinking it unlikely. "It's your life. Just don't move away too far. I'd miss you too much."

"So you don't care if I turned into another Fee?" she stopped dead, rounding on him, heart high.

"You won't, Francesca." He couldn't resist it. He

bent his head and briefly brushed her velvet mouth. Fast and light, still consumed by the pleasure of it. "Remember all the heart-to-heart talks we used to have when we were kids. You want home and family. A man who loves you. A man who is fully committed to you to share your life. And what was it? Four children. That's a full-time job," he added with a sympathetic laugh.

"That's what comes of being an only child," she said as he steered her onwards. "My growing up was painful. I'm not going to let that happen to my children."

"But you still need your mother's encouragement and approval?"

"That's normal isn't it? It's what we all hope for. Parental approval?"

He nodded gravely. "Our parents were one hundred percent behind Rafe and me. Brod and Ally endured a kind of hell. I didn't fully appreciate how deeply your parents' separation affected you until recently. While we're on the subject, what about your father? Would he object so strenuously to your becoming an actress if it ever turned out that was what you wanted?"

"Wow!" Francesca's exclamation said it all. "Actually he'd be *shocked*. Depend on it."

"Because he has big plans for you?" Definitely. It was an inexorable fact.

"They won't work, Grant, if they're the opposite to mine," Francesca murmured, in the fierce grip of sexual longing. "I don't want to disappoint either of my parents but as you've just pointed out my life is my own. That's what makes your pushing me away so peculiar."

"For pity's sake, Francesca. That's not what I meant

at all.'' He stared down at her, her beautiful skin silvered by the moonlight.

"But you won't allow I know my own mind?" Her response was swift.

"What *is* your mind, Francesca?" He made a little grimace, taking her firmly by the shoulders and turning her to him.

"Are we allowed to use the word love here?" A flush of colour had appeared on her cheeks. Even by moonlight he was able to see it. "You hold so much back."

He was haunted by the truth. "There's no way ever, Francesca, I'd hurt you. I'm in love with you," he admitted freely. "You know that. You're in my mind all the time, let alone my dreams." How intoxicatingly erotic he didn't tell her.

"You care a lot but you won't take me seriously." She couldn't control the wave of resentment that welled up.

"That's ridiculous and you know it."

Her chin came up. "Then maybe there's some part of you you don't want me to share. A man like you would worry about loss of liberty, loss of freedom."

He was shocked she thought that. "So what do you want me to do? *Marry* you?" he demanded of the embodiment of his dreams.

"I'm sorry, sorry." Suddenly Francesca broke away feeling utterly humiliated. Where was her pride? Did she really have to force his hand?

"Francesca." He came after her, wrapping his arms around her. "It's never been like this for me with *anyone*. I want you desperately. So desperately I can't really understand myself. That day in the cave, I wanted to take you then. I was a hair's-breadth away from messing up your life. My life. It's not as easy as you're saying. You can't know what's involved.''

''And you won't let me learn?'' The strong passion in him communicated itself to her.

''I'm trying to think what's best for both of us. God, do you think I'm so utterly selfish I'd trap you in a cage?''

She broke away again, moving like a shadow into the swaying sheltering trees. ''I don't want to hear it.''

''You've got to hear what I'm saying.'' He found her easily in the velvet dark, following her fragrance. ''I take the idea of marriage as a very serious business. I'm like the black swans. I'm going to mate for life. If you'd had my own kind of background I wouldn't hesitate for a minute but you were reared to the high life. Do you really think I'd ever let you run off? Do you think I'd ever let you get away from me with another man?

Tears sprang to her eyes at his forcefulness. Didn't he know she loved him? ''I don't know what you're talking about,'' she said, her agitation apparent.

''But it happens, Francesca,'' he groaned, trying to get a handle on an emotional situation that was gaining swiftly in intensity. ''It happens all the time. Not every woman can stand the isolation, the lack of entertainment, theatre, ballet, concerts, art showings, all the things you've been used to, being on your own when your man's away. I have to point out these things. I'd be painting a false picture if I didn't.''

Even as he spoke, trying to warn her, prepare her, he didn't know which, shards of desire were piercing him through, sharper and sharper as she stood quietly under his hands, her long hair rippling over them like skeins of silk. He was desperately afraid of his own driving male hunger so fierce it could frighten her. "Hell I'd take the all-for-love gamble if you could pay the price. If I married you I'd never let you go," he exploded. "Can't you understand all this loving, this passion is dangerous?"

His hands were sending electric currents through her. She loved his hands, the shape of them. Hands were important to her.

Francesca bowed her head in acknowledgment, knowing her feeling for him had not only coloured her world, but turned it on its head. There was a Before Grant and After Grant. What else was Fate for? Nevertheless she turned away saying poignantly. "I won't bother you again."

"Francesca!" he moaned aloud his frustration, torn between stifling her mouth with kisses and letting his ardour cool. Love. This kind of love was like jumping off a cliff.

"It's depressing coming down to earth with a crash." She made a gallant attempt at humour, almost reading his mind. "You're quite right, Grant. We don't have enough in common."

Nothing would work without a solid base of trust and hope.

CHAPTER FIVE

THE week the film people moved into Opal, Grant had to fly to Brisbane for a meeting with Drew Forsythe, set up some time back. A meeting that went so well, it spun out to intensive discussion over a period of three days as Forsythe found time out of his hectic schedule. Both men clicked, sons of dynasties, full of vision, energy and ambition with the brain power to make it all work. So it was working out deals by day, getting the go-ahead from his own financial advisers and at night Drew and his beautiful wife, Eve, made it their business to see Grant enjoyed himself.

They organised a dinner party one evening, and tickets to "Pavarotti and Friends" in concert, the next. They even rustled up a very attractive young woman called Annabel to make up the numbers, dark brown hair, big brown eyes, a head-turner in her own right, but Grant couldn't get Francesca out of his mind. Such was the depth of his feeling for her, she was a constant "presence." Before he'd left she had already been accepted for the role of Lucinda despite Fee's stated qualms. Ngaire Bell and Glenn Richards had swept Fee before them after hearing Francesca read.

"No shortage of talent in this family" was Ngaire's comment, breaking into a big smile. "With Francesca's looks and voice she would never be out of work. With no experience at all she understands the part thoroughly."

"Audiences will weep for her," Glenn Richards

added, looking spellbound. Francesca got such "agony" out of his lines. It was very gratifying.

It struck Grant as ironic Francesca was playing a part that had some relevance to their own situation, however slight. The character in the book, Lucinda, a gently bred English girl migrates to Australia with her handsome, vital, adventurer husband, loving him so deeply she is prepared to give up everything, homeland, family, friends to share his life. Eventually the rigours of trying to survive, let alone cope in a harsh new land with no one outside her husband who thrives in his new environment, to turn to for comfort or advice, wears her down. Never strong, painfully aware of her husband's disappointment in her, his expectations so much more than she can give, her inability to conceive, Lucinda sinks into a depression that ends in tragedy.

"Don't come without a box of tissues," Ngaire warned, using one herself. She was enormously encouraged by Francesca's ability to win sympathy for her character without portraying her as in any way wimpish. Francesca delivered her lines movingly, and with great sincerity bettering the very talented Paige Macauly.

Even Fee had been impressed, in fact her little girl took her breath away. Perversely Fee was hurt. Francesca hadn't asked her to run through her lines with her, or even offer a few words of expert advice.

"Brought it all on your own head, Fifi," David told her. "Francesca wants to contribute. Let her."

Whilst he was in Brisbane, Grant decided to take the opportunity to speak to an architect about his proposed homestead. Drew recommended an excellent man and an appointment was set up by Drew's secretary. The homesteads of Opal Downs and Kimbara appeared in a number of editions of *Historic Homesteads of Australia* and when Grant arrived at the architect's office he found the best coffee table edition lying open on the desk. They talked for quite a while about family influence and inheritance, the marriage between architecture and environment, while Grant revealed the sort of thing he wanted.

He expected the architect, Hugh Madison, a handsome clever-looking man in his late forties to pick up a pencil and tracing paper, instead he went to the computer and immediately began drawing up concepts. It was fascinating watching a wonderful kaleidoscope of graphics, but Grant still preferred drawings like the framed architectural drawings that hung on the walls of Opal. Drawings he had loved all his life. It was agreed Madison should visit the proposed site and a tentative date was set towards the end of the month. Madison would travel to the nearest outback domestic terminal and Grant would pick him up from there and ferry him back to Opal.

"I feel quite excited by the prospect," the architect told Grant as they parted. "It will be a joy! It's not often one gets the chance to design a major contemporary homestead. The powerful mystique of the outback will be inspirational. It will fully test what gift I have." As it would have to, Madison privately thought. This young man radiated purpose and energy. He was also very definite about what he wanted. He would be an exacting client but a very appreciative one if Madison could deliver his dream. Madison was confident on both scores.

* * *

Back at the Opal homestead, Francesca was finding filming wasn't as easy as she supposed. As a novice she had so much to learn, even how to turn her head but Ngaire, the guiding hand, was very patient with her, taking her steadily over her scenes. They didn't amount to many—Lucinda disappeared early—but they were essential to the story. They were shot to surprisingly few takes, sometimes four or five, never as many as Francesca feared might be necessary given her inexperience. But she made sure she came well-prepared— as well-prepared as Fee, who continued to show her amazement at this new side to her daughter.

Ngaire seemed delighted by both their work. She even listened to Francesca's input regarding her own character, a delicate young woman but still possessed of courage, struggling to survive in a world radically different from everything she had known. For all Ngaire's demonstrated brilliance, Francesca found she was remarkably kind and easy to get on with, never once giving way to temper when sometimes, as could be expected, things went quite wrong.

The lights were hot, cords trailed all over the floors. The make-up was just awful. It took such an age to put it on let alone get it off. Wearing the costumes in the sweltering heat. But Francesca found herself having a very good time. The trick was to forget Francesca de Lyle completely. She was Lucinda who loved her husband desperately, knowing each day she was losing him to forces outside her control. A young woman's dreams shattered. A young man's vision rewarded. Francesca was stunned to finish a particularly poignant scene only to see her mother and Ngaire bunched together with tears pouring down their cheeks.

"Oh my God, darling, you could make your mark!"

Fee cried emotionally, neatly evading a whole lot of equipment to take Francesca in her arms. "You do have a lot of your mother in you after all."

Each night when they watched the day's scenes reeled off, Francesca couldn't believe it was herself she was seeing on the screen. It gave her an actual frisson seeing her own face as she had never seen it before. She couldn't help but know her looks were out of the ordinary but the young woman on the screen was lovely in a way she hadn't fully appreciated and she had a way of speaking with her eyes and her hands. It cheered Francesca enormously to know she was acquitting herself rather well. It affirmed her value, reinforced her confidence in herself.

"And with absolutely no experience!" Fee exclaimed, still struggling to come to terms with this unexpected side to her daughter. "Just goes to show the power of the gene. Ally will marvel at this when she sees it."

Except Ally always knew I was a closet actress, Francesca thought. It was different with her mother who viewed her as much more a de Lyle than a Kinross.

Glenn was always there at her shoulder, ready to offer help if she needed it, ready to explain, to instruct, to admire. Glenn was very much part of everything, not only the screenwriter, but Ngaire's much valued colleague. Ngaire and Glenn took their lunch break together, heads close as they got into intense discussion about how things were progressing. In the evening Glenn had taken to asking Francesca to go for an after-dinner stroll with him. Francesca didn't know quite how it happened. Certainly she hadn't initiated anything but she found Glenn attractive, his personality easy yet stimulating. There was a depth to him she liked and they had the film in common as a constant subject of conversation.

"So when is Grant coming home?" Glenn slid the question in neatly the third night out.

"I don't really know." Francesca shook her head desperate for Grant to return home.

"Really? I thought you two were very close." Glenn stared down at her, attracted to her strongly but unsure how to proceed. It wouldn't take a rocket scientist to discern something intangible but very powerful between Cameron and Francesca.

Yet Francesca was startled by the question, not thinking herself and Grant so transparent. It wasn't as though there was any kissing or touching or telling conversation in front of other people. "Surely you've had very little time to see us together?" she parried.

He gave a faint laugh. "I'm someone who notices things, Francesca. I'm a writer. It's my training and my nature."

"So what have you noticed?" She tried to speak lightly.

"I would say you two had a special understanding."

Francesca stopped to shake a tiny pebble from her sandal. "I'm not sure what you're getting at, Glenn?"

His voice was wry. "I suppose what I really want to know is are you spoken for?"

She knew she blushed, grateful he couldn't see it. "A writer must be noted for getting to the point."

"It's not every day I meet someone like you, Francesca," he said. "I don't think it's a secret, either, that I find you very attractive. I would like to get to know you better. But maybe that's not possible?"

How to frame a response? As though it were any of his business anyway. "Grant and I are very good friends." Francesca lifted her head to stare up at the glittering desert stars. Friends? When he filled her with the most wonderful sensation of "coming home."

Glenn evidently wasn't impressed. "Don't you just hate that," he mocked. "Very good friends."

"Well that's all I'm prepared to say."

"Actually I am rushing it," Glenn apologised, shaking his head ruefully. "But a man's a fool if he lets someone wonderful like you pass him by. You're beautiful, Francesca. You're also very talented."

"I'm sure Mamma's surprised," Francesca answered lightly, trying to turn the conversation. She did find Glenn attractive. In some ways he charmed her but there was only one man she wanted and perversely he was trying to push her away.

"Would you think of repeating your experience?" Glenn asked, warmed by the silken brush of her arm.

"You mean consider acting as a serious career?" She sensed he was very interested in her answer.

"There would be much to learn, Francesca, but there's no doubt you're a natural and the cameras love you. It doesn't love everyone no matter how good-looking. I've seen beautiful people film as quite ordinary."

"Strange, isn't it?" Francesca mused. "I suppose it's all about photography. I've always taken a good picture. But to answer your question, I don't want to be a film star, Glenn. That's not my dream at all."

It was absurd to feel such disappointment. "And what is your dream?" he asked, looking down at her silken head.

"In some ways the hardest thing of all," Francesca

responded. "To have a happy, lasting marriage. To raise a family. Bring all my children up with the right values. Help them to become people of confidence and accomplishment. I want to *love* them. Have them love me. I never want discord or alienation. I fear conflict."

This girl had been hurt. Deeply hurt, Glenn thought.

"No easy ambition," he murmured

"I know." She looked back at the purple sky. "But I want to focus all my energies on family. If one is in the fortunate financial position to do so being a wife and mother is a full-time job."

"Fee's career would have taken her a lot away from you?" he said with sudden realisation.

"Yes." Francesca nodded not wanting to discuss the breakdown of her parent's marriage, her father's custody of her which Glenn didn't know.

"But I understand from Rebecca that you had a first-class P.R. job in London?"

"That's true. I was competent but I've said my goodbyes. It didn't make me feel I was doing anything terribly important. There was no *charge*. I wanted to have a musical career at one time but my father vetoed that. It wasn't quite the thing."

"I expect your father wants what you want. For you to marry well and happily."

Though Francesca laughed, it sounded a little hollow. "He has my future husband lined up."

"Good grief you're surely not going to let your father pick your future husband?" That would ruin everything, Glenn thought.

"Of course not," Francesca answered calmly. "But there's been a bit of pressure there. From my side of the family and his."

"Your suitor's?" Glenn was totally distracted.

"It's a class thing, Glenn, being an Australian you mightn't understand. I'm a 'today' person. My father definitely isn't. Being an earl has a lot of implications."

"I would imagine," Glenn agreed dryly, his quirky eyebrows going up. "And being an earl's daughter has its responsibilities, I take it?"

"They do have an effect on me." Francesca remembered all the times she had suffered inner qualms and discomforts, aware of her father's plan for her. "I can't overlook them but my parents had their life. Surely I must have mine."

"I should jolly well say so." Glenn was thinking too much parental involvement was a terrible intrusion on a person's life. "Surely this chap knows you don't love him?"

Francesca's voice was gentle, almost resigned. "I do love him. I've known him all my life. He's counting on that. But it's not that kind of love. That *one* person."

That one person! It sounded very much like she'd found him. "Does Cameron have any idea about all this?" Glenn asked. Cameron was in love with her. He was quite sure of his own radar.

Francesca answered with some irony. "Grant seems to be on side with my father's master plan."

Glenn turned his keen, intelligent brown eyes on her. "I find that very hard to believe. I see Grant Cameron as a tough, very determined young man in a man's world. He wouldn't knuckle down to anyone."

"Except maybe himself," said Francesca.

His father had always told him, especially when he was a headstrong kid. "Don't *do* things, Grant, without thinking them through. Hell, hadn't he learnt? Yet he couldn't wait to get back to her, every day bringing him closer to asking her to marry him and to hell with the rest. Why not let it out? Let his feelings go free? Tell her exactly what he felt for her. Why didn't he simply cry out, "Now I've found you I'll never let you go!" *Why!* Did his love for her run to self-sacrifice? Was that what love was? Putting the loved one's welfare before one's own?

In his business he had grown into the habit of setting down all his concerns, identifying them by putting them in print. Then working out solutions from there. Even as he was hiring an architect to draw up plans for the new homestead his mind was ranging over other options. Other places from where he could operate.

Places where Francesca wouldn't feel quite so isolated and the climate would be kinder. Maybe most of the Camerons from the beginning had been blondes or redheads? They'd had time to acclimatise over the generations. He was as genuinely fearful for Francesca's beautiful skin as a collector would be fearful of hanging a fine painting where it received too much strong daylight. Francesca was taking up so much of his head space he felt he was never without her.

He was flying in over Opal, on a hot clear day, looking down at the great maze of interlocking billabongs and creeks, marked by narrow bands of verdant green on both sides of the water channels. The mulga, the vast region where acacias predominated, spread away to the horizon, bridging the gap between the hardiest eucalypt country and the true desert with its golden plains of pungent, pointed, spinifex and saltbush, its glittering gibber-stones and rolling dark red sand-dunes.

How he loved it! His home. It called to him as it always did when he went beyond its boundaries. The Dead Heart. Only it wasn't dead at all. It was beating, magnificent, unique; the flora without parallel for its adaptation to such a harsh environment. Even the ghost gums grew out of sheer rock where occasional storm waters had flowed and the barren interior became an ocean of wildflowers that gloried in its short, breathtaking tide.

Flowers! The fragrant flowers of the inland. Blazing on and on. Mile after mile. In such a harsh land none had thorns. Neither did the trees and bushes of the desert. Nothing to protect themselves. The exquisite roses had thorns to protect them. In other parts of the world thorns were the rule rather than the exception. Grant went with his stream of consciousness, which always carried images of Francesca. She might have been the only girl left in the world so obsessed was he with the thought of her.

The fair Francesca! A pink rose with satin petals. A rose in the wilderness. Once this wilderness, this great savage land, the parched deserts and plains formed the bed of the Great Inland Sea of prehistory. Twenty thousand years ago the vast Interior had been clothed in luxuriant vegetation to rival the paradise of the wild, the tropical rainforests of the Far North. Crocodiles had once thrived as they still did north of Capricorn. There were many drawings of crocodiles recorded by the aborigines in the rock paintings in and around the Wild Heart. A remarkable witness to the length of time the aborigines had roamed Australia. One of the rarest trees in the world, the Livistona, a tall, graceful tropical "cabbage" palm he had seen growing in pockets in the heat of the desert. A microclimate created by a river gorge.

An oasis in the desert. Ferns and palms and the ancient cycads, their emerald-greens contrasting with the fiery red walls of the cliffs and the deep sapphire sky.

An oasis. Lushness in the arid spinifex plains.

It mightn't be the natural environment for a rose but roses survived and flourished in the sheltered gardens of Kimbara, which relied on bores that had been sunk deep in the Great Artesian Basin. It had taken generations for the gardens at Kimbara to flourish. Generations, a great deal of time and money, a dedication that had filled Kimbara's women's souls.

In his grandfather's day the gardens at Opal had been significant though they had never rivalled Kimbara's. He remembered his mother working hard to keep the gardens going. He remembered her talking about the difficulties. It had taken such a short time for Opal's gardens to die after their mother had been taken so cruelly from them. But Ally would bring them back. Ally was a doer. Ally and Francesca. Cousins. And great friends.

He began to imagine Francesca walking through the gardens love would create in the desert. Francesca in a microclimate. In an oasis of fragrant flowers. Surely if he could create an oasis for her she could not only survive but thrive. Go forward, a voice in his head told him. You can only go forward. You can't go back.

The cast and crew were taking a break from filming when he arrived at the homestead early midafternoon. All these strange people in his family home. But they were paying well and Bush Rescue would get a very welcome injection of funds. Fee saw him first as he pulled the Jeep off the circular driveway into the shade of the trees, waiting for him at the top of the steps.

"Hello there, Grant, darling," she called, the incomparable Fee completely at home in her elaborate get-up that had to be stifling in the heat. "We've missed you. How did it go?"

He bent to kiss the cheek she extended to him, a thin layer of the heavy make-up used for filming smearing his lips. "Sorry, darling." Fee produced a handkerchief from somewhere in her deep violet costume, dabbing at his mouth.

"It's all right, Fee," he reassured her casually. "It'll come off. In answer to your question, things went well. TCR and Cameron Airways are not far away from signing a deal. The lawyers will work it out. Where's everybody?"

Fee gestured gracefully towards the house. "Taking a break. It's hot work as you can imagine, consequently tempers are getting a little frayed. I came out to catch whatever breeze there is. Apart from that things are moving along nicely. Francesca has been the truly big surprise. She's amazingly good."

"Why wouldn't she be?" Grant countered breezily, feeling Fee hadn't been giving Francesca enough credit. "She *is* your daughter."

They were all over the main reception rooms so Grant decided on going immediately to his room, changing his clothes, then looking in on Francesca and Ngaire on his way back. He sent a searching glance through the drawing room nevertheless hoping to catch a glimpse of Francesca. He wondered what she would look like in period costume. That tiny waist his hands could span, her beautiful hair dressed in unfamiliar fashion. He couldn't wait to see her on the footage they had shot. It was a pity he'd had to go off as shooting started but he couldn't have cancelled his meeting with Drew. It was too important.

They were sitting side by side on an old Victorian love seat. Richards obviously feeling the need to hold Francesca's hands in his. He had his dark head bent to her, speaking earnestly, while she listened as attentive as any man could possibly wish. She was the embodiment of Lucinda in her dark grey gown, the bodice tightly buttoned, a show of cream near the throat, the heavy full skirt spread out across the rose velvet. Her glorious Titian hair was drawn back severely from her face from a centre parting with some kind of thick roll at the back. The hair style and get-up reminded him of how they had tried to make Olivia de Havilland plain for the part of Melanie in *Gone with the Wind*. Never succeeding. Both de Havilland and Francesca had such sweetness of expression quite apart from the lovely features that could never be denied.

And just because he was the screenwriter did that give Richards the right to go into a huddle with Francesca? Surely Ngaire, who was nowhere to be seen, should be handling the direction? Grant had thought he would be overjoyed to see Francesca again, thought they would greet each other like they'd been parted for years. Instead here she was lifting her head to stare soulfully into Richards's eyes while Richards stared back at her, clearly under her spell.

What the hell was going on? Grant fumed. Whatever it was it ripped the heart out of him. He broke his glance, striding off towards his bedroom, his earlier mood of excitement and anticipation replaced by one he barely recognised as jealousy. Not that he had time for any of it, he thought grimly. He had work to do.

Bob Carlton was a tower of strength to him but he couldn't leave him carrying the load. Also Bob would be anxious to hear all about his meeting with Forsythe.

Dressed in his everyday uniform of khaki bush shirt and trousers, he went back through the house, hearing voices from the formal dining room he and Rafe never used while they were on their own. Obviously they were back at work. Not that he was about to interrupt. Not now. In his absence he had arranged for one of his men to ferry Francesca, Fee, Ngaire and Richards back to Kimbara at the end of the day's shoot and the leading man when he arrived—he could have for all Grant knew. The male film crew elected to stay close to their equipment, bunking down in the stockmen's quarters, and taking their meals there.

The women, four in all, wardrobe and make-up had taken over a bungalow, which had been made as comfortable as possible by a couple of the station wives. Over the period of time it took to finish the outback scenes, the wives were assisting the camp cook who could produce dishes every bit as good as those many city chefs could offer. Opal staff worked very hard. Opal staff deserved to be fed very well. It was essential to keep up their energy level and good spirits. It was mandatory as well, to ensure station guests were well catered for.

Grant stalked off realising he had to return before sunset if he wanted to see Francesca at all. He had planned on ferrying them back to Kimbara himself but something about Richards's proprietorial attitude and Francesca's seeming quiescence had set him off. It shamed him and made him angry he could be so jealous. A feeling entirely new to him and something he didn't want to accept. He realised with a kind of despair this was another thing that went along with passion. He didn't like Richards's intimacy with *his* girl!

Fee waited until she and Francesca were getting out of their heavy costumes, handing them over to Liz Forbes, from wardrobe, before she mentioned Grant had arrived home.

"You mean he never came in to say hello?" Francesca turned sharply towards her mother, feeling a clutch of dismay on two accounts: Fee had neglected to tell her and Grant hadn't called in.

"I thought he would," said Fee taking off her wig and placing it carefully on the dummy.

"Perhaps he didn't want to interrupt us," Francesca suggested, trying to rid herself of the notion Grant hadn't missed her as much as she had missed him.

"We were taking a break at the time," Fee protested. "Don't be upset, darling." Fee began to brush her own hair out. "He's probably had lots to attend to The meeting in Brisbane went well."

"Couldn't you have told me earlier, Mamma?" Francesca asked reproachfully, not appreciating the fact Fee seemed to be working underground to drive a wedge between herself and Grant.

Fee shook her head. "Darling girl when you're in character it's best not to have any outside distractions. I'm proud of what you're doing. You're very good you know."

But Francesca wasn't to be diverted. "I think you planned it, Mamma." She looked her mother in the eye, seeing no sign of apology on Fee's still stunning face. "You like Grant. At least I thought you did but you're doing your level best to create divisions."

"Darling girl, I'm not the enemy here," Fee exclaimed. "I don't want you to ruin your life." Tears suddenly filled Fee's eyes and she made no attempt to blink them away. "I *do* like Grant. He's an admirable young man but I just can't see he's for you."

"Okay so who is?" Francesca challenged, more aware than anyone her mother could call up tears at will. "Don't leave it up in the air. *Who?*"

"Jimmy," Fee's response was instantaneous as though she'd come up with a crucial piece of information. "Jimmy Waddington. Surely you can't have forgotten him? Jimmy will make you happy."

Francesca concentrated hard on not getting angry. "How's that?"

"Darling, he knows you so well," Francesca cried with more than a touch of theatre. "He *understands* you. You've been great friends since you were children. Be honest now, weren't you in love with him?"

"I didn't know what love was." Francesca shook her head. "I'm very fond of Jimmy but fondness isn't what changes your life."

"Maybe not," Fee admitted. "Being in love is wonderful at the time but it doesn't last. Lord, child I should know."

It had to be said. "I'm not frivolous like you, Mamma."

Fee opened her eyes wide. Francesca didn't realise it but she sounded exactly like her father. "Darling, couldn't you be more respectful?"

"I'm surprised you don't agree. Anyway Jimmy *doesn't* understand me. He doesn't think I have a serious thought in my head."

"What nonsense!" Fee gave the impression she was shocked. "You know perfectly well he thinks you're a wonderful girl. More importantly you have the same background. Your father has hand-picked Jimmy for your husband.''

"Father's not the expert on marriage, either,'' Francesca said. ''Anyway fathers have no right to do that.''

"You can face him with that?'' Fee challenged, locking her daughter's gaze.

"It wouldn't be easy, but yes.'' Francesca gave a long-suffering sigh. ''What are you trying to suggest anyway, Mamma? In refusing Jimmy I'm betraying Father. Is that what you're saying?''

Fee stared off for a moment. ''Please don't raise your voice, darling. Ngaire and Glenn are still about. I'm the last person in the world to want to upset you. I love you, but I must point out Grant in many respects is an unknown entity.''

"After all these years?'' Francesca gave a wry little laugh.

"Darling, you met him briefly when you came for visits,'' Fee pointed out. ''You didn't really get to know one another until recent times.''

"So you don't recommend him as a husband?'' Francesca said. ''Be frank.''

Fee reached into her handbag and pulled out her eau de cologne. ''I'm sure he'll make a delightful husband but maybe a difficult one, too. He's very ambitious. Hungry for success.''

"He's a success already, Mamma,'' Francesca said in a pained voice. ''Grant told me he wants to give something to his country, to his community. I believe him. The Camerons have money already. Money isn't the motivating factor with Grant.''

"Don't be ridiculous, darling,'' Fee said with hard irony.

"I'm not being ridiculous." Francesca shook her head. "Money is fine. Everyone welcomes it but I know Grant means what he says. He wants to do things. He has a vision. Don't please tell me Jimmy has one."

"At least you'll be able to handle him," Fee said in a voice that suggested Francesca wouldn't be able to handle Grant. "Come on, darling," she coaxed as Francesca turned away from her. "I'm sorry if I'm upsetting you but I'm trying to do the right thing. At least give yourself *time*. I know all about dynamic men. They sweep you off your feet, but before you know where you are—"

"Please, Mamma." Francesca signalled she had had enough. "You're so used to thinking of me as your little girl...you can't see I'm an adult. I can't depend on you or Father to make my decisions for me."

"Even when there's so much at stake?" Fee pleaded, using her full voice. "Your happiness? Your well-being?"

"May I speak now, Mamma?" Francesca asked. "Even then. This is the most serious relationship of my life. If I'm ready to take the leap Grant is reflecting on things long and hard. In fact it might ease your mind to know he, too, is considering our relationship might be dead wrong."

Fee frowned deeply as though no one was permitted to think such a thing of her daughter. "My darling, don't you see you could fight about everything! I see a huge contrast between you two," she said.

"Then you don't know Grant or me as well as you think," said Francesca.

* * *

Grant did return to ferry them home but Grant and Francesca never had the chance of a private word until they reached Kimbara homestead and the others had gone inside.

"Couldn't you stay, Grant?" Rebecca, who had been standing with them on the verandah asked. "Do you have to rush away?"

"Actually I do, Rebecca." Grant softened his refusal with a smile. "I have to be ready for a big job on Laura tomorrow. Thanks anyway. Give my best to Brod when he comes in. Tell him everything went well."

"That's great. I know he'll be thrilled for you." Rebecca smiled, a sparkle in her eyes. "I'll leave you two to catch up. You're coming to Fee's book launch aren't you?"

"Well I'm thinking about it," Grant said.

"You *have* to!" Rebecca insisted. "It'll be lovely for the four of us to go out together one night while we're in Sydney. You and Fran. Brod and I. See if you can pull out all the stops."

"I'll try!" Grant sketched her a salute. "Rebecca is looking radiant," he said, when he and Francesca were alone.

Francesca raised a delicate eyebrow. "Is that really so surprising? She's head over heels in love with her husband."

"Then she has excellent taste." Grant allowed his eyes to dwell on her. The slant of her blue eyes, the curve of the lid, the line of her cheek, the clean cut of her jaw, the exquisite shape of her mouth. She'd creamed off all the heavy film make-up and her beautiful skin had a slightly shiny lustre. "How are you?" he asked, wanting to tilt her face to him and kiss it. Amazed he didn't.

"A bit down in the dumps," Francesca admitted. "Why didn't you come in and say hello when you arrived?"

He raised a sardonic eyebrow. "Because I didn't want to interrupt your little coaching session with Richards."

"You're kidding!" Whatever she imagined, it wasn't that.

"Never more serious actually. I glanced into the drawing room only to find the two of you on that old love seat, tenderly holding hands."

"Could it be your eyes were deceiving you?"

"No."

Francesca glanced up at him quickly, her eyes searching out his mood. "If it were anyone else but you I'd say you were jealous."

"Not overly. You don't think I'm capable of being jealous?" he asked, iridescent eyes narrowing over her.

"You wouldn't allow yourself to go so far. Now let's see. We were sitting on the love seat. I'm trying to cast my mind back."

"Cocooned in your own little world," he prompted. "Richards has his head bent to you. You were staring up soulfully at him. It was one hell of a scene!"

It must have been to cause such a reaction. "Now I remember. I'm just a beginner, Grant," she explained patiently. "Green as they come. There's so much I don't know. Practically all of it. Glenn has been very kind to me."

"Kinder than Ngaire?" he asked suavely. "I thought she was the director. Isn't it her task to correct any mistakes? Smooth over all the little rough bits."

"Ngaire helps me as well," she told him briskly. "Everyone does. They give me all the support I need."

"So you're loving it then?" Because I missed you like hell.

"I think I'll look back on it as a very worthwhile experience," Francesca said. "But I'm not taking it too seriously. And what about you? I want to hear all about your meetings with Drew. How's Eve by the way? Did you manage to see her?"

He nodded. "Eve's fine. She sent her best regards. They entertained me royally. Two nights. A dinner party at their beautiful home. Then Pavarotti and Friends in Concert. Our meetings went very well. Drew and I are on the same wavelength. Let's walk down to the chopper?" He took her arm, wondering how things could go so easily wrong, when he desperately wanted to hold her close. "I called in on an architect while I was there. Drew recommended him."

Her head seemed to explode with stars. "Really? Now you know something funny? I dreamt that you did."

He squeezed her delicate upper arm. "Francesca you're not *acting?*"

"No I'm not. I don't tell fibs. I actually did dream w—" she could hardly give herself away "—you and an architect were speaking together. It was quite a vivid dream. I've thought about it a lot. As a matter of fact I've had a lot of fun sketching some designs. You might like to see them some time."

"Run and get them now," he said. "I'll wait."

The high colour of excitement came into her cheeks. "I want us to look at them *together.*"

"Then come back to Opal with me tonight," he said with quiet intensity. "I want to be near you. Make love to you. Open all the doors and curtains so the moonlight will fall on your beautiful, luminous skin."

She hesitated, half-poised to run back to the homestead. "Sometimes you're crazy."

He gave her an ironic look. "You don't want to come?"

"You know I do." Her breathing softly rasped. "I missed you terribly."

"Did you?"

"Yes."

He took her chin and tilted her mouth. "Poor, poor, Francesca," he said very softly. "It was no different for me."

She stood very still while he kissed her, feeling the force of his desire held on a tight leash. "What is it you want?" she whispered into his mouth, half-closing her eyes.

He wanted to slide his hand down over her swan's neck, cup her smooth, creamy breast, feel it swell to the tenderness of his fingers. He wanted to let his hand descend...

"Just one word, Francesca," he said huskily. "*You.* There's so much I want to tell you."

"So much I want to hear."

Anything might have happened next, so closely were they drawn together in heart and mind, only Fee chose that very moment to come hurrying out onto the verandah, walking to the balustrade. "Darling, Ngaire wants to show us today's rushes. Sure you can't stay and see them, Grant?"

Grant's smile was openly mocking. "I really have to get away, Fee." Of course she knew he did, if he wanted to be on Opal by nightfall. "You'd better go, Francesca," he told her dryly. "Fee's full of surprises. Now she's applying a bit of maternal pressure."

Goddammit, yes, Francesca thought in amazement.

The phantom mother of her childhood, the brilliant shooting star, was now siding of all things with the ex-husband she had so capriciously cut out of her life. Nevertheless Francesca sprang to Fee's defence so deeply was the habit ingrained. "Mamma only intends to be…"

"Please don't say kind," Grant warned, his strong, handsome face showing its high mettle. "I think Fee could be a ruthless opponent. What she doesn't intend is for you to be buried away in the wilds. Not that I blame her. God knows I can see both sides."

Gently, conciliatory, Francesca touched his hand. "I'll bring my sketchbook over tomorrow. I so much want to show it to you. Another part of my dream—" the *same* part…she didn't tell him in her dream the homestead and the garden merged "—we were planning an oasis in the vast landscape. It would be impossible to conquer such immensity but one could devise a sort of sweeping Australian garden landscape. Something on the grand scale to live in harmony with the unique environment and survive drought. I suppose it's far too ambitious, but one could landscape some of the watercourses. Indigenous trees of course but massed plantings. And there could be a polo field with lots of shade for the ponies, the spectators and their cars. It would be an enormous challenge, probably daunting, but so exciting. We could create our own vision rather than going along with existing…"

He interrupted her almost fiercely. "We? You did say *we*, didn't you?"

Francesca didn't falter, even with her mother waiting anxiously for her up on the verandah. "Yes," she answered, her heart in her eyes.

CHAPTER SIX

NEXT day he couldn't get away from Laura Station until after the midafternoon break. He had a new recruit on roster, a man the same age as himself, Rick Wallace—an excellent helicopter pilot with more than enough qualifications and flying hours to warrant his inclusion in the team, but a mite short on actual experience in aerial mustering. It was his first priority as boss of the team to make sure Wallace was handling the job properly. He always conducted a premuster briefing, always took aerial shots, pointing out possible dangers on the site, sometimes acting as copilot to continue with the first-hand instruction. By smoko he was sure he was leaving the rest of the day's work in Rick's gifted hands. Rick was well on the way to having the same sort of skills as himself and he, too, was mad on flying. They would be friends.

When he arrived back on Opal it was to find the leading man had arrived to film his scenes; Ngaire introduced them, pleasure in her eyes. Her hero was an up-and-coming young English actor unconventionally handsome, dark-haired, light-eyed, with reputed considerable sex appeal for women and the ability to get male audiences onside. Grant knew the role called for a genuine English accent rather than an assumed one, which could slip from time to time, as well as a male lead with an international "name." The name was Marc Fordham. He had a friendly manner and a firm hand shake. Grant liked him.

Marc was dressed in part in a stained and dusty rather billowy white shirt and tight dark brown trousers and a wide silver buckled belt. His dark curly hair was shoulder-length and tousled, a few days growth of beard on his face. He looked great, every inch the dynamic hero of the novel. The women wouldn't be able to take their eyes off him, Grant thought, amused the dark tan—dark as Brod's that went so extraordinarily well with light eyes—was courtesy of the make-up department. Someone would have to warn him of the dangers of the outback sun. Though he tried not to make it too obvious his own eyes were going in search of Francesca. Finally when she didn't appear and he couldn't sight her, he was forced to ask Ngaire where she was.

"Out riding," Ngaire volunteered, as though it was her own greatest pleasure to be in the saddle. "With Marc here we thought we'd go ahead with his scenes with Fee." Fee played the hero's distant relative, the wife of a powerful Sydney landowner keen to recruit the hero to his interests. "Francesca wasn't needed so she and Glenn decided to go for a ride. Glenn is a weekend rider," Ngaire laughed indulgently. "Francesca, I believe is a brilliant horsewoman. One of the many reasons she got the part of Lucinda. She has that mad, suicidal ride in her final scene. We'll leave that to the last days of shooting. We were even going to ask you if you could line someone up for the long shoots. Someone who could pass for Marc. Marc has had to learn to ride a horse of course, but he's no expert. If you could come up with a stand-in?" Ngaire looked winsome, clearly hoping or counting on, either he or Brod would do it. But he couldn't answer for either of them.

Instead he nodded noncommittally. "Any idea where they're headed?"

"Oh, not too far I would imagine." Ngaire started to lose interest, keen to get on with filming. "Francesca said you liked her to stay close to the home. I think she left a note for you." She cast her eyes around, saw nothing, fluttered a hand. "She was sitting out on the side verandah, sketching as I recall. Maybe it's out there."

No note. A number of sketchbooks tidily stacked on the circular table, a leather case full of pencils, charcoal sticks close beside. He was finding out something new about her all the time. It was absurd to be jealous of Richards. Beautiful as she was, Francesca as a femme fatale he couldn't buy. Francesca was honest and true. She had gone for a ride and she would be back soon. Grant sat down taking the sketchbook from the top of the pile, conscious of a swift emotional response as his eye fell on a drawing of...

Himself. Or himself as Francesca saw him. He stared at it for a long time thinking she had made him look a whole lot better looking than he was, maybe a touch arrogant with the lift of his chin and the angle of his head. But it was undeniably him and it was very good. He turned more pages marvelling at the drawings. Himself again and again. Members of the family. There was Brod, a genuinely handsome devil. Beautifully lily cool Rebecca in any number of poses. Fee in an armchair, Fee reading a script, Fee and David, numerous sketches of Ally, a few of Rafe looking like a medieval knight. Perhaps that was the way she saw him.

Other books were devoted to animals, beautiful drawings of horses, cattle, kangaroos, emus, brolgas, swans, pages of the giant wedge-tailed eagle with detailed inserts of wings. She was wonderful at capturing animals in action. She must have sketched at the instant it happened. Other sketchbooks contained Kimbara landscapes, with stockmen at rest, or driving herds of cattle. There were innumerable little sketches of wild-flowers, lilies, ground orchids, boronia, flowering vines.

Another couple of sketchbooks were devoted to studies in anatomy the structure of the human body. They appeared to be absolutely accurate. Other exercises fleshed out the skeleton. Obviously Francesca had received a good deal of training. He'd no idea she was so talented in this way. He wondered if she painted in other media—watercolours, pastels, oils? He would love to see what she could do. Talent like this deserved the greatest encouragement.

The very last book in the pile, almost hidden, contained what he was so desperate to see. Francesca's visions of his dream homestead. The first sketch was front on. So real he felt he could reach out and open the front door.

Francesca! He loved what he saw. She drew effortlessly as if she loved it. The facade was completely modern, huge areas of glass that could be opened to the desert air. The central core of the homestead enclosed front and sides by sweeping verandahs, no flamboyant classical columns but representations of narrow steel supports running the entire length of the facade. A concession to tradition a double height entrance but what totally blew him away rising behind it a three-story open bell-tower, modelled on a Spanish mission tower from where bells would call and one would have a fantastic view of the desert landscape.

Other drawings followed, different aspects, different

angled facets, various sketches of the tower, all a little
different, open views down into the interior with the
layout of open-plan rooms and an enclosed central
courtyard with a tall fluid water sculpture instead of the
traditional fountain. But what was so fascinating was
Francesca had put splashes of colours—yellow ochre,
burnt umber, raw sienna, ultramarine blue, cobalt blue,
cadmium yellow and red, lamp black, he read them
off—down the side of the pages along with specified
materials, stone, glass, steel, richly grained timbers, different shades and textures of granite.

Obviously their minds worked in the same way.
Working quite independent of him, with her own background of a jewel-like English country home, she had
come up with a design structure little different from his
own except for the novel addition of a tower.

It was downright uncanny. Her vision reflected his
own. A graceful house for all its modernist approach.
She had even sketched entrance gates to the main compound. Not high to restrict the uninterrupted views but
substantial, making a statement, two low pillars of desert rocks anchoring bronze gates depicting two magnificent rearing horses, the whole shaded by an
A-framed roof from which hung the legend, Myora-
Opal Station.

There weren't words for what he felt. He only knew
he wanted to live there. With the girl of his dreams,
Francesca.

This was the kind of thing he had wanted from the
architect but he realised in that he was being too sim-
plistic. Madison had picked up on all his basic cues,
his vision a striking contemporary version of the traditional homestead but Francesca with her knowledge

of the site had worked from the imagination. Clever, clever, girl.

From his vantage point on the verandah he was the first to see the grey gelding come in, disconsolate, head down, reins trailing.

God!

Grant vaulted up from his chair, taking the steps at a single leap, running across the garden to the open grasslands. The horse heard his repeated whistles, carried on the wind. It pricked its ears in the direction from whence they had come, then adjusted its direction. Minutes later Grant had it by the reins. The grey's coat was covered in sweat. It was obvious it had bolted, only slowing its flight when it was in sight and sound of the homestead. It gave Grant considerable comfort to know Francesca was a fine horsewoman with hands like silk. But Richards, according to Ngaire, was an inexperienced rider. He only hoped if it was Richards who had become unseated he'd been wearing one of the light weight helmets the station insisted their guests wear. Galloping across the plains with only an akubra to protect a fragile skull was only a romantic notion for anyone but a skilled rider.

A young aboriginal boy came running as he approached the stables complex, taking the grey's reins. "What'sa matter, boss?" Bunny so called because of his prominent but dazzlingly white, front teeth stared up at him with black, liquid eyes. "Where this one come from?"

"You tell me, Bunny," Grant responded grimly. "Were you on hand when Miss Francesca and her friend went out?"

"Sure was, boss." Bunny was happy to confirm it. "Saddled up for them. Miss Francesca picked out

Gypsy. A bit frisky but I reckon she can handle 'im. The guy settled for Spook. Nice and quiet." Bunny ran an ebony hand over Spook's side. "Though with a horse you never to know. Reckon he's come a way. Sweatin'."

Grant looked as if he was about to curse but didn't. "So someone has taken a tumble I just hope to God, Bunny, you gave him a hard hat?"

Bunny looked him straight in the eye. "I was goin' to, boss, but Miss Francesca insisted on it right away. Wore an akubra herself like the rest of us. Talk about bushie!"

"You know she's half Australian. Get the saddle off him, Bunny," Grant said. "Any idea where they headed?"

Bunny waved a hand. "Miss Francesca didn't say and I didn't think it my place to ask."

"That's okay," Grant said. "See ya, kid. From now on you have my permission to ask everybody where they're headed. So don't have any qualms. I'll go back to the house and check. Miss Francesca was supposed to have left a note."

Fee as it turned out had it, which struck Grant as odd, given Fee appeared to be against his and Francesca's deepening involvement. She apologised profusely when Grant told her crisply she should have handed it over once he returned.

"One of the horses has returned without a rider," he told her, grey-green eyes glinting. He took the note from its unsealed envelope and opened it. "Don't panic, it's not Francesca's horse," he had the grace to reassure Fee. "She was riding Gypsy. Richards was riding the grey gelding, Spook. It's a quiet work horse, but like all horses it's unpredictable." As he was speaking he was reading swiftly. "They've headed out to Blue Lady Lagoon. An easy trail. I'll get going."

"I do hope it's nothing serious." Fee was looking unaccustomedly chastened. "I understand Glenn was little more than a beginner. He couldn't handle anything at all lively. And Francesca! I know she's got a lot of common sense but I hope she gave that serious consideration."

"I only hope we're not looking at broken bones. Just in case I'll have to put out a call to the Royal Flying Doctor."

"Glenn wouldn't have a clue about roughing it," Fee said.

"Would Francesca?" Grant countered briskly. "Anyway I must go. There's only so much daylight left."

He took the four-wheel drive, heading out across the plains country to a favourite haven for all the station, black and white. Blue Lady Lagoon. All the stations in the Channel Country had similar flowering waterholes, filled with beautiful waterlilies, the sacred blue lotus, the pink, the cream, the rarer red lotus and the giant blue waterlily of Blue Lady Lagoon with its spectacular flowers growing up to a foot across. No matter how hot it was Blue Lady Lagoon with its tall trees, numerous golden grevilleas and native hibiscus, its understorey of mosses, vines and ground orchids offered an almost junglelike cool. He could understand why Francesca had headed there. He didn't realise it but he had tightened his jaw until it ached. He wouldn't accept Francesca was perfectly all right until he laid eyes on her. At least they couldn't get lost. They had only to follow the chain of billabongs home.

Ten minutes out he was confronted by an extraordinary sight. In the shimmering, dancing light of the atmosphere a small figure appeared out of the near distant mulga. The figure was on foot leading a black horse that could only be Gypsy. Hunkered down over the horse's back was a far more substantial figure. Richards.

Without further ado Grant tore off across country, angered beyond words—Francesca was walking in the heat. No way to travel! God she could have been walking for miles! If so she would be parched. A wave of hostility towards Richards swept through him, rivalled by his great sense of relief. Richards had to be in a bad way if he had consented to do the riding while Francesca walked.

Closer he saw Francesca had come to a standstill, holding firmly to Gypsy's reins, looking up at Richards probably asking him how he was. Moments more and he brought the Jeep to a halt, jumped out and moved towards them with all the speed and purpose of a big cat.

"What's happened here?" His intense scrutiny devoured Francesca as he checked to see if she was all right. Only then did it move on to Richards as he tried to neutralise his anger. "Are you okay there, Glenn?" he asked, moving alongside Gypsy soothing him.

Richards managed a smile, trying to straighten. "Afraid I took a tumble." That was clear from all the grazing down one side of his face and the condition of his clothes.

"No bones broken." Francesca came to stand at Grant's shoulder. "He's concussed, I imagine. Very groggy."

"So you let him up on your horse?" He all but accused her in a display of perverse male emotion.

"Come off it, Grant. I had to," she answered in a mild voice. "He's in no condition to walk."

"And *you* are?" He stared down into her lovely, sensitive face. She was wearing her wide-brimmed akubra with a light blue bandanna protecting her nape, but her face was very flushed and beads of sweat had gathered across her forehead at her temples and beneath her eyes. Sensibly she had let down her long hair as a curtain and had rolled down the long sleeves of her yellow cotton shirt but he could plainly see a runnel of sweat moving down between her breasts with damp patches all over the blouse and waistline. "The first thing we've got to do is get you a drink of water," he said harshly, starting back to the four-wheel drive.

"It's all right." She came after him to lay a reassuring hand on his arm. "I made sure we didn't set off without water. I stopped to give us a drink just before we moved out of the scrub."

"So you can drink some more now," he said, making short work of pouring out some water from the supply in the vehicle.

"You're not going to stand over me while I drink it?" Francesca asked wryly.

"Yes, I am," he answered firmly. "Something else I want you to do while I get Richards is put this towel over your face and neck." He started to saturate a small hand towel with water, not content with handing it to her but taking charge himself. He swept her akubra off then began sponging her hot face with the cool, clean water easing part of it around her throat. "What boots have you got on?" he demanded next, his brow knotted.

"Good ones," she gasped as he ceased mopping her

up. But her sense of being dreadfully overheated had eased.

"So get in the vehicle," he ordered briefly. "I'll attend to Richards."

Francesca did so gratefully, making a real effort to appear sprightly though it cost her a lot. Glenn might be very gifted in his own area but a man of action he wasn't. The last hour had been fairly ghastly as she made their way out of the rough country where the gelding's startled gallop had ended, and found a track through the mulga until they reached the open plain. Nothing had spooked the grey gelding outside its rider. Glenn simply didn't have sympathetic contact with the horse. In fact he had all the common faults, especially with his hands. A horse's mouth was soft and sensitive. Glenn's handling harsh and unencouraging. She'd even been giving Glenn riding instructions as they went, realising he'd never been taught, much less got to the point where he understood horses. Nearing the lagoon despite her objection, he had resorted to force instead of hands to change the gelding's direction, kicking the heel of his boots into its side.

Spook didn't like that. Francesca the horse lover didn't blame him. With Glenn's armchair seat and his bad leg position it was inevitable he would be thrown. To make matters worse he had complained about wearing the helmet from the outset saying he found it much too hot when he really wanted the breeze through his hair. Somehow she had persuaded him to keep it on until they reached the green shade of the red river gums. There he had whipped the helmet off with a kind of bravado, ignoring her pleas to keep it on.

The miracle was she didn't have to pick up the pieces after he'd been thrown. Some facial grazing where he'd hit the ground hard. A large lump on his head, all the symptoms of concussion, blurred vision, grogginess, some retching. She'd had the devil's own job getting him up on Gypsy, finding the right boulder to use as a mounting block, then using her own weight on the other side to counteract his. Finally it had all come together without strain to the horse. Gypsy, the ex-racehorse, had been very, very good while the inferior hack, Spook had taken the rare occasion to play up.

Her clothes felt terribly damp and heavy on her, her shirt soaked from Grant's ministrations, her hair slick with sweat in need of a shampoo. She turned back the cuffs of her shirt, rolled them up then she whipped off the wet blue bandanna. Her heart was still thudding in her chest after her long walk but she just had to grit her teeth and bear it until she could get under a lovely cold shower. Originally she had wanted to ride to the homestead for help but Glenn though disorientated had been adamant she didn't leave him. She might be getting used to vast distances and life in the wild but Glenn appeared to be genuinely intimidated by the bush. In his altered state he gave the impression he really believed if she left him he'd never be found again or dehydration would claim him.

With Glenn comfortable in the back of the vehicle, Francesca wasn't surprised when Grant shot her a rapier glance. "Why didn't you ride for help, Francesca? You made it so hard for yourself walking in." He noted with relief the high colour of exertion had faded a little from her face. In fact though she was uncharacteristically dishevelled she was looking remarkably calm and composed.

"My fault, I'm afraid," Glenn mumbled from the

back. "I wouldn't let her go. I don't mind telling you I find the bush extremely intimidating. It's great size! A man doesn't realise until he gets out here."

"You're sounding better, Glenn," Francesca said with satisfaction, turning her head with its dark curtain.

"What a fool you must think me."

Why not? Grant thought with strong disapproval.

"I have to say you did give me the impression you were a better rider," Francesca pointed out in a wry voice.

"But, Francesca, I thought I *was*. Just goes to show how much I'm out of my element here. I've been on horse riding trails. Come to think of it, it was mostly in a straight line and always with a party."

"And what became of your helmet?" Grant asked gratingly, trying to push his extreme irritation with Richards to the back of his mind. Not only had Richards expected Francesca to sit and hold his hand, he had expected her to lead him seated on the horse across the spinifex belt in the heat of the afternoon. He'd never have allowed a woman to undertake such a long, hot trek. This was rough open country not a jaunt through a tree-filled city park.

"It came off in the fall." Francesca aware of Grant's anger risked a fib. "The safety harness must have worked loose."

Grant sighed. "Tell me another one."

"Sorry. I'm ashamed of myself. Glenn was feeling the heat. He took it off briefly to cool down."

"And what spooked the gelding?" His eyes sparkled. "Make my day and give me a straight answer."

"It was the darnedest thing." Glenn found his voice from the back. "Such a tame horse yet it cut up a treat. I gave it a little bit of a kick in the sides to make it change direction and ended hanging on for dear life. It bolted into the scrub. I felt a branch might take off my head."

"Especially without your helmet," Grant murmured dryly. "They say all's well that ends well, but I don't suppose you'll be interested in going riding again." He mightn't have put it into words but *not with Francesca* came over loud and clear.

By the time they got back to the house everyone had been alerted to the situation, swarming out onto the verandah as Grant drew the four-wheel drive up at the base of the front steps. There were hugs and kisses all round. As the injured party, however self-inflicted, Glenn came in for the lion's share of attention but as Fee drew her daughter away her face revealed the strain of the past half hour.

"My darling!" One good look was enough for Fee. Embarking on a horse ride with Glenn Richards had not paid off. She could see Francesca's pink shirt was drying quickly in the heat otherwise she looked as if she'd been dunked, her beautiful long hair pressed flat against her skull her face carrying an expression Fee remembered down the years. Francesca trying very hard indeed to be a good little girl and not cause any fuss.

"It's all right, Mamma," she was saying now, anxious to offer reassurance. "Glenn took a tumble but no bones broken. A bump on the head and a modicum of hurt pride."

"To hell with that!" Fee laughed shortly, looking back over her shoulder to where Glenn was seated on a verandah chair with Ngaire and the crew in attendance. "I don't know why you took him in the first place. All Glenn knows about horses is what he's learned in the movies."

Grant pondered that. "I've never seen the hero look for the little lady's help. He *rode*. *She* walked," he said, trying with some difficulty to lighten his own expression.

"For crying out loud." Fee shook her head in a flurry of ringlets. "Look, I've got to have that out with him." She made to stalk off with a considerable air of majesty, only Francesca caught at her arm pleadingly.

"Please don't, Mamma. It wasn't as though Glenn was himself. He'd taken a tumble. I expect quite a lot of bumps and grazes will appear overnight. "He was far too groggy to walk. The gelding simply bolted for home."

Outback-bred Fee stared at her perplexed. "But my darling child, why didn't you simply leave him there and ride for help?"

"Because he got quite agitated when I tried to leave."

"A case of a city man behaving rather badly in the bush," Grant offered in a sardonic voice. "Leave it, Fee. Glenn has a nice little story for after dessert. Right now Francesca should get under the shower and cool off. She had quite a trek in the heat."

Fee knitted her brow very delicately to lessen the chance of wrinkles. "There are things that *need* saying, Grant."

"Don't be upset. Forget it, Mamma," Francesca begged, hearing another wave of laughter at Glenn's droll account of his tumble. "It was all my fault. I knew almost from the outset Glenn had little experience. I should have abandoned the ride altogether."

Grant agreed with a single, very definite nod. "By

the same token a man of sense would have told you how little experience he'd had.'' He reached out and encircled Francesca's fragile wrist. ''I can find you a clean shirt of mine to put on. Sorry about the jeans. You can use either the bath or the shower in the master bedroom. I'll find you some clean towels. Richards can use the shower room off the storeroom at the rear of the house. There are clean towels there. I'll get Myra up to take a look at him.'' Grant referred to the wife of Opal's overseer, for years a qualified nursing sister. ''I don't think there's much the matter with him if he can sit around spinning yarns.''

''I'm going to make it my business to put them all straight later,'' Fee promised. ''I'll come with you, darling,'' she said to Francesca, feeling for once extraordinarily useless.

''No, Mamma, I'm fine!'' Francesca shook her head. ''I just want to cool down. Thank the Lord I was wearing a good sun block. Glenn will find himself with a bad case of sunburn, but I'm afraid he was too careless for comfort.'' She glanced at her watch, then back to her mother. ''You're not finished for the day are you?''

''We'll see, darling.'' Fee glanced around. ''We were doing some lighting set-ups when that wretched horse came in. But now that you're both home safely I expect Ngaire will want to finish the scene. Marc and I are ready. He's a pleasure to work with. So professional.''

''Can you pass on that message to Richards, Fee?'' Grant asked, as Fee started to move off. ''I'll put a call through for Myra to come up to the house and take a look at him. She'll find him a good spray for that sunburn. It doesn't matter how many times you warn people of conditions out here they don't seem to take much notice."

All the rooms at Opal were of a generous size but the master bedroom was huge, dominated by a beautiful satinwood four-poster the floral pelmet of the elegantly decorated canopy matching the chintz of the ruffled bed valance that fell to the carpeted floor. All the furnishings were instantly familiar to Francesca's English eyes, the George III giltwood mirror, the mahogany chests, the scrolled day bed near the French doors, a pair of Regency chairs. All of it could have come from Ormond even to the side cabinet painted Chinoiserie panels and the English needlepoint carpet. Obviously the Camerons had gone "Home" to do their buying or had the furnishings and all that went with it shipped out.

"The bathroom is through here," Grant said, leading her through the dressing room to a very large bathroom, which had been modernised without losing its sense of the traditional.

"You wouldn't have anything like shampoo?" Francesca asked hopefully, realising the master suite hadn't been used for some time.

"I wouldn't think here," Grant said doubtfully, looking towards a wall of handsome timber cabinets and matching wall cabinets complemented with brass fittings. "But let's see, Rafe and I didn't want a live-in housekeeper like the old days. A couple of the station wives, headed by Myra, keep an eye on the place for us." As he was speaking, Grant walked to the line of cabinets trying the wall fixtures first.

"It's your lucky day," he announced, full of satisfaction. "There's a whole range of stuff here. There could even be towels in the linen press. Myra must be anticipating the day Rafe and Ally get home.''

That was evident judging by the contents of the tall linen press that flanked the cabinets. Francesca saw two of the deep shelves held bed linen, others a selection of towels in three colours: white, pale yellow and apple-green.

''I don't know what we'd do without Myra and her crew,'' Grant said gratefully. ''They're downright motherly. I expect Ally will change things but she'll always have their support. So what's it to be.'' He turned to Francesca as she stood staring around her.'' Bath or shower? I can run the bath for you if you like? You might relish a soak.''

Francesca raised her eyes to his, finding them electric, sparkling with erotic fantasies that rivalled her own. ''I would but I think I'd better settle for a shower,'' she said as calmly as she could. ''Easier to shampoo my hair. Besides you'll want to get everyone home before sunset.''

''I find I'm more concerned about you,'' he said, still gazing at her with those gold-flecked eyes.

''The shower is fine, Grant.'' It shook her that she was wishing he could join her, her whole body, tired as it was, vibrating with awareness, her pulses speeded up.

''All right I'll leave you to it.'' Grant moved abruptly, prey to his own wishful thinking. ''Thanks to Myra everything you need is there down to new combs. Take your time. Some of those towels would be bath sheets. Rafe and I hate those little bits of things that would only go once around you. You'll be able to wrap yourself up.''

Without a backwards glance he moved off, closing

the bedroom door after him with a soft thud. Alone Francesca shook her head, trying to clear it. It was truly extraordinary the way he affected her. She had never in her life believed herself to be highly sexed. Now she realised it was only because she had never met the man who could deeply stir her. The master musician who could play her like golden sounds.

Quickly Francesca stripped off her clothes and wrapped herself in a huge yellow towel. Then she walked out to the enclosed verandah off the bedroom where she lay her clothes over a couple of chairs that still received hot rays of sunshine. That should dry them off! Back in the bathroom she flung off the towel stepping into the large shower enclosure that would easily accommodate two people with its frameless translucent walls and porcelain fittings. She turned on the taps, keeping the temperature initially lukewarm. The shower cascaded like a waterfall from a very effective wide nozzle producing a wonderfully, sensual, soothing effect. She held up her face to it letting it splash all over her skin. She really needed this. She had come over really rough terrain on foot and no one could understand the effects of the blazing outback sun, the dazzling quality of the *light* unless they had experienced it.

She reached for the shampoo and conditioner in one, lathering her hair twice then rinsing off. Only then did she start to feel the effects of her trek or maybe it was the alternate play of warm then cold water. A faint mist, like a veil, seemed to rise before her eyes and the legs that had pumped so strongly across the spinifex plains began to feel extraordinarily weak. She made a big effort to pull herself together, lurching forward to grasp the porcelain controls. The mist wasn't clearing.

It was turning into a fog. Surely she wasn't going to do something silly and faint? She hadn't done that since childhood when she had taken a nasty fall from her pony.

Moaning aloud, Francesca made another attempt to get out of the shower enclosure, only barely aware of a tall figure that loomed up outside the glass door.

In the west wing of the house, Grant had put a call through to the overseer's bungalow, glad Myra was around to pick it up. Quickly he explained what had happened to Richards asking her to come up to the homestead and check him over. That out of the way he thanked her for looking after the homestead so well, particularly for stocking the bathroom in the master suite. It had proved a godsend.

Afterwards, with Myra's bubbly, pleased laugh still in his ears, he hunted up a fresh shirt for Francesca to put on. He understood she would be the most fastidious of young women. Of course he was a good foot taller and maybe four stone heavier but the shirt would be clean and fresh and she could turn up the sleeves, tie up the tails, whatever women did with men's shirts. Difficult to fit her out with jeans, he thought with a wry grin, but her pink shirt had taken the worst of it.

A soft collared white cotton sports shirt with a blue stripe through it came to hand. He couldn't remember the last time he had worn it if he'd worn it at all. Either way it looked pretty new or it had been beautifully laundered and pressed. It would do nicely. He had a clear mental picture of how Francesca would look in it. *Only* it. An image that caused him to take a deep, whistling breath. He tapped on the master bedroom door and received no reply. Unless she'd been very slick about it, Francesca would still be washing her hair. The shirt over his arm he trod quickly to the foot of the canopied bed, intending to lay the shirt on the quilted damask coverlet before beating a retreat when he heard to his alarm the most piteous low moan.

The hair on the back of his neck literally stood up, his stomach muscles contracting sickeningly. For God's sake what was the matter? He shouldn't have left her. He should have sat right outside the door.

"Francesca?" Grant strode to the entrance of the dressing room, noting the sliding door to the bathroom wasn't fully shut. "Francesca?" His voice had picked up considerably in volume and intensity. What the hell *was* this? She had to hear him.

No answer but he could hear the water running. He called her name one more time coming right to the sliding door. Another of those moans saw him flinging it back so hard it rocked in its tracks.

Her naked body was even more beautiful than his imaginings, the curves and the contours, the breasts like fruit. She was hunched over the taps, slender arms extended to turn them off, fingers tightening but ineffectually.

"All right, I'm here!" Grant moved with speed, opening the shower enclosure, catching the spray, grasping her with one arm while the other made short work of turning off the taps. "Francesca!"

She slumped against him causing a great surge of desire he couldn't possibly control, her lovely creamy flesh under his hands, breasts so pretty they left him breathless, the lick of red-gold at the base of her body. Desire he was immediately ashamed of. She was fainting right under his eyes.

A long arm with its whipcord muscles shot out and

grabbed a yellow towel. With the utmost dexterity he wound it around her as carefully as if she were a new-born babe, cradling her, before he lifted her completely into his arms, carrying her back to the bedroom where he sat her upright on the side of the bed.

"Francesca, sweetheart!" Quickly he pushed her head to her knees, one arm around her strongly and within moments he was rewarded by the little sounds she made as she came around fully.

"I nearly fainted." Her voice was weak and husky.

"Don't talk." A few moments more and he let her head come up slowly, her long hair hanging in dripping coils. "I'm furious with myself for leaving you," he admitted. "Thank God I came back. How do you feel?"

The first shock over, Francesca started to realise her situation. "Still a bit giddy."

"Hell!" he said quietly. Now that she was recovering he was back to being excruciatingly aware of her nakedness, trying to keep his eyes on her beautifully shaped legs, imagining his hands stroking their satin length. Petite, she was perfectly proportioned, the most graceful nude a master such as Renoir might have painted, though there was far less of her than his usual voluptuous young models. But the red-gold hair, the extraordinary luminescent flesh, the rose tips of her breasts gave off the same erotic charge. The yellow towel had slipped almost to her waist and he pulled it back up with great delicacy, his sense of touch never more pronounced, never more sensuous, her free-flowing hair fell forward over her shoulders and down in the curve of her back, so richly coloured it lit her skin.

"Myra is coming up to the house to take a look at

Richards," he told her gently. "I think I'll ask her to also take a look at you."

She was trembling slightly, a mixture of emotions spiralling through her, not able to handle any of them. "I'm all right," she protested, shaking her head a little so spray fell on him.

"I'll get her to come all the same. It won't hurt." Grant stood up and walked through to the bathroom coming back with a fresh towel. "Here, let me dry your hair."

She held the towel tight against her breasts. "I'm dripping all over the coverlet."

"Who cares! You don't suppose Ally is going to leave any of this intact?" he asked wryly. "Sing out if I'm hurting you."

Hurting her? Every sexual nerve end was screaming into life.

Yet she sat quietly, the yellow bath sheet wrapped tight around her while Grant drew her hair back over her shoulder and mopped up the long ends. Then he applied the towel with a more vigorous motion until it was ready to comb. He might have been doing this all his life so efficiently he went to work drawing the wide-toothed tortoiseshell comb down the full length of the strands until the job was done.

"Have you any idea how young you look?" He forgot everything and put his mouth to her tender nape.

Her whole body began to tingle, responding irresistibly, causing her to lean in against his lean powerful frame.

"What are we doing here?" he whispered into her ear, one hand coming down to cup the delicate mound of her breast. "You should be getting dressed. I should be going for Myra." His head dipped further, his mouth against her ear, the top of his tongue flickering over its shell-like shape. "Francesca!" He began whispering things, endearments that turned her heart over, his breath warm and clean going deeper and deeper into her, like a tunnel that reached into her soul. "You taste of fruit," he marvelled. "A delicious white peach."

She thought she would faint again with the pleasure of it. The ravishment.

"God, what's the matter with me?" he whispered hoarsely something about the attitude of her body concerned him. He lifted his mouth away from her with a remarkable effort. "I'm sorry, you need care not hungry kisses." His voice was so low and seductive before it turned brisk and businesslike. "If you hold the towel around you I'll help you get into my shirt. That's what I came for. Here, Francesca." He reached for his white shirt, slid it on one slender arm, fixed it around her back, then pushed her arm into the other sleeve.

She didn't feel able to help him and he seized her hand and kissed it. Then he went down on his haunches in front of her, beginning to do up the buttons, hazel eyes smouldering as his hands skimmed her breasts, slid along the smoothness of the fine cotton, lingered in her lap, the warmth of her, the place where he wanted to be.

"Well that's done!" Her weakened physical condition was the only thing that saved him. He wanted her so much he could feel his own head swimming. Only then did she make eye contact.

"I love you, Grant," she said, more sweetly he thought than any other woman would have said it before.

"Will you say that when you're ready to say your goodbyes to me?" he asked her tenderly, his whole soul crying out for her. "I bet you never even told your father about me."

It was true. It never seemed to be the right time when she rang home. Her letters contained a lot of news: people, places, families, her own family the Kinrosses, and their neighbours the Camerons. But unless her father was excellent at reading between the lines he would have little idea she had fallen madly in love with Grant Cameron. Why didn't she tell him? Was she a coward? She only knew her father had always been there for her when her mother wasn't. She dreaded the thought of hurting him, a beloved parent, shattering his dreams.

"Somebody ought to tell him, Francesca," Grant warned. "Tell him straight, you owe him that. If you can't. *I* can. Then you'll really know what to expect."

Her delicate fingers touched his face, tracing the cleft in his chin. "How would you tell him?" Was he offering a magical solution?

He made a little sardonic grimace. "What do you think, flower face, I'd hop on a plane."

"Just like that?" His decision seemed to galvanise her.

"Why not?" Your father doesn't bother me. He bothers *you*. He even bothers Fee who doesn't give a damn about anyone. I suppose that's what comes of being a belted earl." Grant stood up determinedly. "Now I'm going to get Myra to take a look at you. Why don't you lie down while I'm gone."

"I'll take the daybed near the door." Francesca made an attempt to stand up, Grant assisting her until she was upright. Her feet were aching, she realised without surprise. But what about her neck and her back? How had she hurt herself? The answer was obvious, struggling with Glenn, first to get him off the ground then mounted on Gypsy. Strangely she hadn't felt much of anything at the time. She was going to have to suffer for it now. But she had no intention of complaining. It wasn't her way and she had brought a lot of it on herself. She should have left Glenn to go for help. Even as she thought it she knew she would do the same thing all over again. Ally always told her she was a softie.

She looked utterly adorable in his shirt. It was miles too big for her, but for all that or maybe because of it she looked as innocent as a child. Yet incredibly sexy. The flame-coloured mane he had combed back from her face and over her shoulders was drying in the late-afternoon sun. It radiated light, the perfect foil for the creaminess of her skin. She touched every part of him, the sight of her an actual hand squeezing his heart.

He took her chin between his fingers, tilting her face to him, staring into those starry eyes with a very serious expression. A total acceptance of his role. "I want you more than I've wanted anything in my whole life," he told her, his voice harsh with emotion, but reverent. "I've dreamed about you. Night after night after night. I want you in my bed. I want to take your precious gift of virginity. And it is a gift, Francesca. I want to be the only man in your life. *Ever.*"

The whole room seemed to be filled with the fabulous colours of the sunset. Tears came from a deep place inside of her. "And I'm yours to keep. To have and to hold."

Triumph blazed in his eyes. His arms closed around her so strongly they almost lifted her from the floor. He found her upturned mouth, a smile of utter bliss at its corners, her tongue feverish to mate with his. The kiss went on forever. "Do you love me?" she whispered frantically, twisting away from him for a few seconds. "Say it. Say it."

"*Say* it? I'll show you." His whole body was reverberating with passion. There was no alternative left in the world for them but marriage. And God how he wanted it. He would do anything for her. Fly to England. Seek out her father. Speak to him. Ask for his approval. He owed him that courtesy. With Francesca by his side he could build something of great value. She needn't jettison her old life altogether. He would always allow her to visit her father, her homeland, her friends. Hell he'd find time to go with her. She was the only woman who would make his life right and he was drunk on her love.

Fee calling in to see how her daughter was, found her and Grant locked in a kiss so passionate she felt no one had the right to intrude on such intimacy. But disturb them she must, discovering in herself a great rush of regrets. Although she had known Francesca and Grant were in love she'd had no real inkling of the depth of their feelings.

What she was witnessing was something irrevocable. Something that would work. A cataclysm of desire the likes of which she had never thought her lovely young daughter capable. Francesca was so young, so inexperienced, sheltered all her life. Now it seemed Grant Cameron had taught her all about her own sensuality. This wasn't the holiday affair she had feared. Francesca's loyalty lay with Grant Cameron when Fee genuinely believed it lay elsewhere.

While Fee stood rigid, unable to move, Grant and Francesca finally became aware of her presence. They didn't spring apart. They didn't act in the least guilty.

They broke apart slowly. Francesca shook her long hair back from her face and Grant gave his white mocking smile.

"Fee, you've made an art form of exits and entrances."

If she'd been thirty years younger Fee would have blushed. "Sorry, I didn't mean to intrude but I thought at least Francesca you'd be lying down. And what on earth have you got on?" She peered at her daughter's petite figure, astonishment on her face.

"Goodness, Mamma, can't you see?" Francesca came forward for inspection, the most beautiful smile blooming on her face. "It's a man's shirt. Grant's."

"And it looks very fetching," Grant remarked, reaching for Francesca's hand, a unity of two. "Actually, Fee, we made a mistake leaving Francesca. She all but fainted under the shower."

Fee who couldn't even remember all her lovers' names looked and sounded aghast. "And you rescued her?"

"Thank God I was on the spot," Grant answered very seriously. "I returned with the shirt and heard Francesca's moans."

If it hadn't been her own daughter, Fee would have come out with something possibly caustic, instead she rushed to Francesca's side. "Is this true, darling? You're such a delicate creature."

"Even Ally might have fainted after a trek like that," Grant offered dryly.

"I don't think so, dear," Fee said. "Ally wouldn't have been fool enough to take pity on the man."

"Lucky Ally to get your approval, Mamma," Francesca said with a gentle touch of censure.

"Oh, you know what I mean!" Fee cried. "Don't

be miffed at me, darling. You're such a tender-hearted little thing.''

A wry smile spread across Grant's face. ''And there is the shining fact, she makes no fuss. None of us have heard a word of complaint from her. Francesca may be tender-hearted and I love her for it, but she knows how to handle herself. Tell you what. You two have a talk. I'll go fetch Myra. Francesca is looking a vision at the moment but we can't overlook the fact she did go into a faint.''

''For a girl who nearly passed out you're looking the vision Grant said,'' Fee commented, looking into her daughter's eyes. ''You've come to an important decision, haven't you?''

''I knew right from the beginning,'' Francesca answered simply. ''Grant had certain fears for me. As you did, Mamma, and probably still have. But ours won't be a marriage between two very different people. A marriage between two cultures, two different lands. Grant and I are soul mates. We agree on mostly everything. All the important things anyway. Now he's finally realised I will be able to adapt to his world. Something I've known for years. I've loved my mother's country since I was ten. It speaks to me, too.''

Fee thought for a long time. ''I should have seen that, darling,'' she said, ''but as usual I was too self-engrossed.''

''I know in my heart, Mamma, this is right. Grant and I will aid each other. He trusts me. He respects me. He knows I can help him. That's the way of a real marriage.''

Fee touched her daughter's cheek with love and uncharacteristic humility. ''Do you realise how lucky you are, darling? It's taken me half a lifetime to find my other half. David loves me just the way I am. Your father desperately wanted me to change. Still he mattered a great deal to me at one time.''

"He loved you, Mamma," Francesca pointed out gently, ever loyal to her father.

"They all did, darling," Fee argued, juggling all her memories, "if I say so myself I was very hotly desired.''

"So am I." Francesca gave her enchanting smile, moving over to the daybed near the French doors and sinking back on it. "I want Father to give me away. I want to go forward to my new life with my hand on my father's arm.''

"Of course, darling," Fee agreed. "But you must tell him about Grant without delay. Once he sees how happy you are I'm sure there will be no anger, no pressure." Fee sincerely hoped not, finding solace in the knowledge the earl doted on his daughter. Besides, stacked up against Jimmy Waddington, Grant would emerge the overwhelming winner.

"As it happens, Grant wants to fly home to see Father," Francesca was saying, sounding as though her own resolve had firmed considerably. "He wants to speak to Father himself. I'm not afraid they won't get on. In many ways Father and I are very much alike.''

"You do show your lineage," Fee agreed. "Little bits of us both you carry around with you.''

"And I'm going with him," Francesca said. "There are many things I want to explain to Father. Many things to thank him for. As for Father and Grant! I think they'll find plenty to talk about," Francesca said prophetically. "There's nothing to stop him coming to see us from time to time.''

"My darling, count on it," Fee said. "Especially when you have your first baby."

Both women laughed, a wonderful companionable sound.

When had her daughter turned from a charming child into a woman ready to take on the biggest challenge in life, Fee thought. Quite obviously when I wasn't looking.

CHAPTER SEVEN

TEN days later with the outback location shots completed and Francesca's small part in the film over, Ngaire, Glenn and the crew, returned to Sydney taking Fee and David with them. Fee still had some scenes, shot in and around Sydney, to go and she needed to prepare for the big party she was throwing to launch her biography. That was set for the end of the month.

"Thank you for saving my life, Francesca," Glenn exaggerated suavely on departure, taking her hand and pressing a lingering warm kiss on it. "I can't wait to see you again at Fee's party. You were absolutely perfect as Lucinda. The best we could have hoped for."

Ngaire agreed with a hug and a kiss. "Let's face it, darling, you could have a career if you wanted it."

Not when I have a better one in mind, Francesca thought, keeping her own big news for the time quiet.

Grant watching Richards turn on the charm had the satisfaction of knowing by the next time Richards saw Francesca she would be very much engaged. He had the ring in his pocket. It had only arrived the day before. And it was breathtaking! Fit for a princess. He'd faxed the family jeweller over a week ago, listing his requirements. 18ct white gold set with a finest quality diamond. Maybe 1.5 or 1.6cts—he left it to them—thinking a 2ct central stone would be too big for Francesca's small, elegant hand. The central diamond was to be flanked by something different. Rare pink diamonds? Perhaps pear-shaped? He drew a sketch of what he wanted, the cost coming in as a secondary consideration. His gift to her had to be just right. The ring was to be exquisite. As flowerlike as Francesca herself.

The jeweller lost no time at all sending a return fax with two detailed sketches featuring a classic central stone, one oval, one round, flanked by the finest quality Argyle pink diamonds. In the second sketch the pink diamonds were pave set. He knew immediately which one he wanted. It all but fitted his own design except for the oval-shaped central stone, which looked better than his own idea of a round cut, the flanking pink diamonds set like leaves. He felt charged to the hilt, desperate to slide it on her finger.

"Rebecca has asked me to stay to lunch," he told her as they watched the charter flight lift into the peacock-blue sky. "After that I have to get back to Opal to supervise a maintenance check." He lowered his head, his eyes beneath the wide brim of his akubra, glittering like gemstones. "What if we take a quick run out to Myora? I want to show you something."

She looked at him with pleasure. "That will be lovely! I've been meaning and meaning to show you my sketchbooks but with all the rush of the filming there hasn't been much time. Fee kept them hard at it. She wanted it all over before the book launch. And you haven't really answered the question. Are you coming?"

"I insist on coming," he said dryly. "What with Richards still acting loverlike. Who said he could press kisses into your hand?"

"Didn't mean a thing," she teased.

"I hope so, I'm amazed by his cheek."

*   *   *

Ten minutes out on their cross-country drive they stopped to watch a pair of roaming emus, one of the world's largest birds, conducting a comic mating dance. The male was acting up so crazily, kicking up its long legs, crossing them, lifting itself off the ground, Francesca couldn't stop laughing. The female on the other hand was displaying a considerable hauteur that could have passed as indifference, stalking about the male or preening her mass of feathers, the assumed indifference as it turned out far from the case.

"Just giving him the run-around." Grant grinned. "Emus are remarkable creatures and not only for their speed. They can find a living in the most arid parts of the run but they seek shelter in thick scrub when they're nesting. The eggs are huge as you know. They require more than two months incubation."

"That's a long time for poor Mum."

"Poor dad don't you mean? The male undertakes that task."

"Well, good for him. Mother kangaroo at least carries her little ones in her pouch. They're just adorable, the joeys. It's absolutely fascinating watching a herd of kangaroos bounding across open country on their long hind legs yet when they walk slowly they use their forefeet and their tail to steady them rather like a tripod, as the hind legs come forward."

"You've made quite a study of them." He didn't tell her he had seen her wonderful sketchbooks. Not yet. She had the eye of the artist. The capacity for acute observation.

When they arrived at the site for his proposed homestead, they could see in the distance a large herd of cattle feeding on the purple flowering succulent, the parakeelya, peculiar to the sandhills. The stock could live on this or other succulents for months without water.

"Rafe and Ally will be home soon," Grant said quietly, still sitting behind the wheel of the Jeep.

"They're disappointed they're going to miss Mamma's party," Francesca said, "but she put the launch off long enough to fit in with filming."

"*And* her marriage," Grant drawled.

"She and David don't want to tie the knot without Ally present." Francesca gave him a quick smile. "Mamma and Ally are very close."

"Does it bother you?" he asked gently, relieved when she shook her head.

"Not really, I love them both. Mamma understands Ally better than she does me. I'll have to get married to convince her I've grown up."

"As long as you don't make it *three* times." Grant had a wry joke at Fee's expense. "Let's get out." He moved swiftly around the vehicle to help her, taking her hand, loving the way she twined her fingers through his. In front of them Myora glowed a fiery red under the hot sun, the breeze that seemed to have sprung up out of nowhere causing a strange sighing sound to emanate from its hollowed out cavities and caves.

"Voice of the spirits," Grant said, looking down at her. "Are you scared?"

"Why wouldn't there be spirits," she said. "This is an old old land, full of Dreamtime significance."

It was time to tell her. Here in this place so close to their hearts.

"I saw your sketchbooks."

She lifted her head, blue eyes surprised. "Why didn't you tell me?"

"I think I was too moved by them," he answered

simply. "I didn't want anyone else to look at them. Or your sketches of *our* homestead. That's something uniquely ours."

"You liked them?" She stared back at him steadily.

"I loved them, Francesca," he said, his dark voice deep. "As I love you. I can't possibly draw like you but you read my mind. Your sketchbooks finally convinced me you truly love this country. The flowers and the animals you've drawn so accurately. Your idea of an oasis in isolation proves how closely our minds work."

She touched his golden face tenderly, in absolute love. "It means everything to me, Grant, you feel like that."

"I do." His strong arms encircled her. "Forgive me for ever doubting you couldn't adapt to a strange land. It isn't strange at all. It's part of the richness of your inheritance. And now I have something for you." He cast his eyes around, settling on a large boulder, mainly rust-red in colouring but with thick yellow ochre veins. "Come sit over here."

"What is this all about?" She let him lead her, feeling unbelievably precious to him. It was wonderful. Intoxicating. As necessary to her as the air she breathed.

"You'll see," he promised.

When she was seated he went down theatrically on one knee before her, flashing her his brilliant smile. "Lady Francesca de Lyle I beg you to marry me. I adore every hair of your Titian head. I'm even prepared to beard your father, the earl, in his den. I want his consent for us to marry. I want his blessing. I want everything that's going to make you happy. We can be married in England if that's what you want. I know you'll want your father to give you away. I'm certain it would please him. I'm equally sure he'll want it that way. I'll risk the grey skies and the cold of your winter. I'll risk everything if only you'll marry me. And just so you won't keep me on my knees too much longer I'd be honoured if, in the meantime, you'd wear my ring." He took a small navy case from his pocket, opened it and withdrew the ring. "Your hand, my lady." His smile deepened as he registered the joyous anticipation on her lovely face.

"Take it," she breathed, feeling her hand nerveless.

He did so, slipping the diamond engagement ring down over the satiny skin of her finger. "Not bad! A perfect fit. I love you, Francesca. I'll love you always."

"Oh, Grant!" she whispered, extending her hand to the sun, watching all the brilliant flashing lights. *Pink* diamonds! So beautiful.

"You're not going to cry, dear love?" Grant asked very tenderly, feeling extraordinarily emotional himself.

"Of course I'm going to cry. It's obligatory on these occasions. Tears of joy!" She flung herself forward, against his chest, his arms closing around her before he lost his balance. They both rolled on the pure clean sand that was covered in parts by a broad-leafed vine.

Now she was gurgling with laughter.

"Stay still. I want to kiss you." He arched over her.

"I haven't told you if I'm going to marry you yet."

"Tell me *after*." He moved with big cat grace, bringing his hands in tightly to hold her body captive, riveted by its *female* suppleness. Then he lowered his head.

"Ah, Grant...."

The laughter died. There was such burning desire in

his voice and in his eyes she felt an answering flame lick her veins.

He kissed her into breathless submission, pressing the length of his body against hers. "Anyway I'm not going to take no for an answer." His fingers tripped the pearly buttons of her shirt and slipped inside, shaping and caressing her naked breast. He was utterly sure of her, the dominant male, but she loved it. Her arms slid around his neck, her fingers digging into the tawny hair that curved thickly into his nape. He was a beautiful man. Beautiful!

"I love you."

"I thought you did," he said passionately.

"I can't wait to marry you."

"I can't wait to marry *you*," he groaned, falling back on the sand beside her. "We have to see your father. We have to make him delighted with our news. A wedding has to be arranged. How the hell am I going to be able to manage all that without ravishing you?"

"But I *want* you to." Her voice choked on emotion. She ached for him to take her.

"And I going to." He was breathing harshly, his handsome, high cheek-boned face taut and hungry but with a strength that confounded her. "But not like this, my love. The first time we're together is going to be very, very, precious. The first time I lower myself into your body. The time and place will be right. No hurry."

"You're too sure of yourself, Grant Cameron."

He turned and kissed her again, brushing back the hair that fell about her face in wild disarray. "I have some news for you that you will like," he told her as they eventually lay back entwined. A small grin crooked the corners of his shapely mouth. "I'm having that architect I saw come out here to walk over the site. It's all organised. We'll show him your sketches. Let him work with them. I'll order it so we can have a three-month honeymoon. Anywhere in the world you want to go. Fiji, Patagonia, Antarctica, the Swiss Alps. By the time we get back, our dream home will be built.''

EPILOGUE

THE Cameron-de Lyle wedding took place in England in June of the following year. The ceremony was held in the centuries-old village church of St. Thomas, adjoining the bride's father, the earl of Moray's splendid country estate in the rolling hills of Hampshire; the reception for two hundred people held in giant white marquees erected in the grounds of Ormond Hall the de Lyle ancestral seat, which at that time of the year were breathtakingly beautiful, a landscape gardener's dream and inspiration. The wedding said to be one of the most beautiful of the decade was covered by *Tatler*, *Harpers & Queen* and the *Australian Woman's Weekly*, so there were plenty of photographs for those who followed the social pages and weren't fortunate enough to get an invitation.

A marvellous shot of bride and groom looking gloriously happy appeared on the cover of the Australian magazine. Although the bride Lady Francesca de Lyle, dubbed by the Australian press, "The English Bride," was indeed English on her illustrious father's side, her mother was the internationally known Australian born actress Fiona Kinross who had had a brilliant career on the London stage, spanning some thirty years. Fiona Kinross, Mrs. David Westbury, was a member of the prominent landed Kinross family, daughter of the late Sir Andrew Kinross, a legendary Australian cattle king, whose forebears had pioneered the industry in colonial days.

There were colour photographs of the bride on her own, looking exquisitely romantic in delustred duchess satin, the sweetheart neckline and bodice decorated with beautiful corded lace that ran down the full skirt. On her head she wore a flaring waist-length tulle veil held in place by a delicately beautiful family tiara of diamonds and pearls. Pearls with a diamond pendant at her throat, a small posy of beautiful white roses in her hands.

There were photographs of the bride with her two small flower girls, an enchanting shot; the bride with her attendants, the stunning Alison Cameron, nee Kinross, matron of honour, first cousin to the bride on the mother's side, Lady Georgina Lamb and Miss Serena Strickland, the bride's friends from childhood, all in harmonious shades of pink silk. There were photographs of the groom with his attendants, the best man, elder brother, Rafe, master of the Australian historic cattle station, Opal Downs, their close friend and recent brother-in-law by virtue of Rafe's marriage to the stunning matron of honour, and *her* brother, Broderick, master of the equally famous Kimbara Station. Mr. Kinross's beautiful wife, Rebecca, was clearly from the photographs some months pregnant but radiant in a simple, elegant blue dress with a gorgeous blue hat.

There was a lovely photograph of the bride with her father, the earl of Moray, both beaming with delight. A photograph of Mr. and Mrs. David Westbury, Mrs. Westbury wearing the most fabulous emerald hat and silk two-piece suit, shoes and handbag precisely matched. No photographs of the bride's father and mother together. But one of the earl with his present countess, Holly. Some photographs of people the

English side of the family didn't know at all. Among them Miss Lainie Rhodes from Victoria Springs, a cascade of blonde hair and an irresistible big smile wore an elegant white-and-navy suit with a rather wonderful confection in navy with a huge navy-and-white bow on her head. "It's wonderful! The best fun!" Miss Rhodes went on record as saying. Seated beside her, a rakish grin on his mouth, a strikingly handsome young man who bore a decided resemblance to the tawny haired groom and his "golden" brother. Family, of course—Mr. Rory Cameron, world traveller.

The honeymoon, which included a flight over Antarctica said to be "truly awesome" in the true sense of the word, would take the happy couple to places as far away as Scandinavia and Canada where the groom wanted to look up members of the Cameron clan who had migrated there in the early days.

It was the perfect day for a perfect wedding, all three magazines reported. Sky-blue and golden the sun pushing its way through a few early-morning clouds to shine down on the happy couple. Everyone who was there and those who devoured the magazine photographs afterwards, agreed it was plainly a love match.

Wasn't that just wonderful!

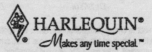

Harlequin Romance®

Experience the ultimate desert fantasy with this thrilling new Sheikh miniseries!

Four best-loved Harlequin Romance® authors bring you strong, proud Arabian men, exotic eastern settings and plenty of tender passion under the hot desert sun....

Look out for:

His Desert Rose by Liz Fielding
(#3618) in August 2000

To Marry a Sheikh by Day Leclaire
(#3623) in October 2000

The Sheikh's Bride by Sophie Weston
(#3630) in November 2000

The Sheikh's Reward by Lucy Gordon
(#3634) in December 2000

Available in August, September, October and November wherever Harlequin Books are sold.

HARLEQUIN®
Makes any time special.™

Visit us at www.eHarlequin.com   HRSHEIK2

HARLEQUIN

Duets™